J D

BLACK CARD

BLACK

Sometimes, all that healing, understanding, and
forgiving feels like an excuse for people to get away with
what they did to you.
No more high roads.
No more "being a better person".
Fuck healing.
Fuck being reasonable.
This book is about revenge.

CONTENT WARNING

CHAPTER 1

She was in her dreary season; a time of year she tracked with the same regularity as fall or winter. It would start on different days and end roughly whenever the hell it pleased, but Essie could count on it towards the end of July—late August, if it was being stubborn.

Thick, grey clouds would drift over her days as summer began its final bid for life that year. As sunsets died brutal—struggling deaths across the sky, each red orb fighting to stay afloat before setting with bitterness—casting long, lanky shadows on the still hot streets of her Kentucky neighborhood, a grimness would slip behind her, grasping her wrists and whispering sweet melancholy into her ear. The words would slither into her eardrum before expanding parasitically, intertwining with her bones. Sadness seeped out of her pores, regret took shelter in the roots of her hair.

She'd move a little slower.

The days would feel *just* a bit more tiring.

Her patience would thin out until every minor annoyance became sharper, more savagely irritating.

Food tasted blander, as if everything needed a touch of salt.

It always began slowly, so that she could fight it and feel a flickering, cruel belief that maybe she could stave it off.

That was the trying period.

A time when you lean your head back too far to laugh too loudly. When you catch someone's joke and choose to chuckle instead of having it pleasantly pulled out of your lungs. Listlessly trying new books, new shows, and new music. Clutching at escapism like rungs on a ladder you were failing to hold onto. Can this miniseries spark-spark and jump-start her happiness? Will *this* book series drip-drip enough dopamine to drown the depression growing inside her?

Music grew tinny in her ears and sunlight started feeling like a glare rather than a kiss.

You'd catch her on a random Tuesday evening in July, going for troubled walks in her neighborhood. The kind of walks that brooding teenagers went on. Essie walked with her head down, hands shoved deep in her pockets, wearing a hoodie despite the heat, watching her shoes leap out and slap the pavement.

The thoughts were the usual thoughts. If her depression were a season, then these thoughts were dead leaves. They fell off in bursts, three to four brown-grey thoughts, dry and begging to be burned, piling on her.

They had the texture of truth and the allure of the intrusive. Like the little ghostly impulse voice that told her to stick her hand into fire—just to see!—or saw train tracks and wondered briefly, how it would feel to lay down and be erased.

Your husband is a stranger. You recoil when he tries to touch you. You dread pulling into the driveway of your own home and seeing his car there.

These ideas would careen in and she'd field them, catching each one in her hands, examining it like it was a rare bug before casting it aside easily.

But during the trying period, one-two would be three to four, then four to five, then six quickly became nine thoughts like that and nine became, *oh god oh why did I marry* him *why am I* here *what became of* me?

So,

Walks.

It was on one of these walks—past trimmed lawns and pastel houses with brown shingles and two-car garages, past front lawn sprinklers and gleaming SUVs—that she saw a black van screech to a halt in front of the Gibson house. The dingy cargo van with rust spots along the trim clashed violently with Kara Gibson's green shutters and pink tulips in the front garden. The van had a loud muffler, which gurgled loudly in the quiet suburb.

The door slid open and from her view from the corner,

Essie saw a woman with a black bag over her head being dragged out of the van. Three men in masks and gloves carefully placed the woman on her lawn, and one of them unsnapped a knife.

Essie reached for her phone, swiping for the dialer to begin calling 9-1-1.

The man cut the woman's hands free and took the bag off her head.

It was Kara Gibson.

Kara Gibson, who hosted barbeques in her back garden by the pool. Kara Gibson, married to Greg Gibson, who worked as a lawyer in the city.

The men gathered around Kara as she stood and embraced each one of them. She began to walk to her front door when one of the men reached out and swatted her ass.

Essie heard her giggle and say loudly, "Keep it up and I'll have you kidnap me again."

The men laughed. They waved cheerfully as they each climbed into the van and sped away.

Kara crossed her yard quickly. Her clothes were in tatters; the white blouse was torn open in the back and flapped in the wind. Her hair was frizzy and stuck out at odd angles. She walked stiffly, as if she were very sore.

At the door, she fumbled for her keys, dropped them, bent over to pick them up, then froze. She whirled around, looking down the street. Her eyes swept over to Essie, still holding her phone, the numbers 9 and 1 already dialed, her thumb hovering over the final digit.

Kara stared at her for a long pause. Then she firmly shouldered her front door open and went inside.

4

Essie thought about telling her husband.

There was a moment, after the door clicked open and before it snapped closed, as she kicked her shoes off and wandered down the hallway towards his computer room, where Essie thought she could.

There was a tennis court of silence between them and maybe she could serve this enticing green ball of gossip over the net. Ryan could swat it back. "Really?" he'd say. "Three men? In a van?"

She'd volley back. "It was like something out of a movie, I swear. She was all tied up, with a bag on her head."

"Should we call the cops? That sounds insane."

There would be interest in his voice. She would be edging into the room and sitting naturally in the little chair next to the desk. His eyes would leave the computer screen and find hers. He'd make a joke. Tendrils of connection would begin reaching out and joining hands over the chasm between them.

Because they'd have something to talk about.

The door snapped closed, and she lingered in the threshold of the room, watching the slant of his neck and the slight bend of his ears under his glasses.

"Hey," she offered. A weak serve. Why didn't she sprint in and begin chattering? Why did everything feel like it had to be scheduled or announced—every moment of intimacy organized by committee to avoid a fight?

Ryan grunted.
She frowned.
No tennis today.

CHAPTER 2

Carly, though.

Carly she could talk to.

When Essie and Ryan had first moved to this neighborhood, she'd had a stark fear that her social life would die a slow, strangled death. It would be relegated to talking to people online, switching deliriously from app to app to keep up and keep in the loop with friends from school, friends from her hometown, friends from the city she'd lived in before Ryan.

Everyone in the community seemed to be a mother, working on their Fisher Price empire. Assembling an arsenal of lawn toys and sneakers, backpacks and sippy cups. Essie watched them hauling thick, grey car seats and folding wheeled nightmares they called strollers.

If they weren't moms, they were aggressively career-oriented. Hillary Clinton's with dyed hair and high heels, stomping out the door each morning to their gleaming chariots. Fem-soldiers of marketing, HR, and management. They trickled into the city to work at tech startups and offices, everyone doing vague jobs they tried to explain at the summer barbeques but failed to communicate what they actually did. Essie would listen, wanting desperately to be like them—they seemed so purposeful, like they had been air-dropped in already *knowing* how to live.

But what if they were wrong? What if they were secretly just as unhappy as she was?

"I would rather smoke weed and be bitter," Carly said one night on her back porch as they derided their entire neighborhood with the gleeful joy of finding someone who hates something just as much as you do.

Carly was like her tattooed older sister—a grim, cynical but ultimately caring friend who was distrustful of everyone as a rule, and frowned on anything too many people were doing. She confessed—that same evening—that she didn't think anyone was truly happy. "Everyone is working very hard at their illusion, and some of us are better at it than others."

"I'm terrible at it," Essie replied.

Carly blew smoke through her nostrils. "That's why I like you."

So, naturally, she had to tell Carly about Kara Gibson and the Three Men. It had taken a mythic quality, like Goldilocks and the Three Bears. This half-certain fable of suburban drama.

After a pitiful night's sleep and a long, dreary day at work, she went over to Carly's. Like solemn statues claiming their posts, they took their usual spots on the porch, sliding into the white deck chairs that were pockmarked with black scorch marks from Carly's cigarettes. Carly sparked her lighter and Essie pulled her legs off the ground to perch cross-legged.

"So tell me again what you saw," Carly said.

Essie launched into it, fishing for every stray detail and iota of information she could pull from the brief image she had. The men, Kara, the van.

Carly made her tell it three times, an interested gleam on her face as Essie recited it. She bit her nails as she listened, and when Essie was done, she let out a long laugh. "Kara *Gibson?* Our cute little neighbor—," she pointed to her house, "—she let me borrow her fucking crockpot? That neighbor? You're telling me she was in a… bondage orgy?"

"That's not what I said. I don't know what I saw. I don't know if I should tell anyone."

"Of course, of course." Carly grinned around the butt of her cigarette. "You told me, though."

Essie smiled. "Obviously. I had to tell someone."

"Not your husband though."

There was nothing to do with that comment but give the same bitter shrug she'd been doing for a while now.

How's your marriage, Essie?

Who fucking knows.

Carly patted her knee. "Don't worry, apparently you're not the only one not telling their husband everything. I'm guessing Mr. Gibson has no idea what his wife is getting up to."

"Should we tell him?

"I'm not getting involved. Fuck that." Headlights slashed across the night, illuminating the backyard briefly. Anderson, Carly's husband, was home.

"Are you telling him?" Essie asked.

"Andy? My luck he'd want to try it," she said dryly, snuffing the cigarette out. "Would you do it?"

"I don't even understand what they did."

"Right, but you have an imagination. Would you get in the van with them?"

"Would you?"

"Probably." Carly avoided her eyes and examined the bite marks on her nails. "Today I did so many mundane things. I stood in line at the post office. I stopped at seven red lights. I made pasta. I'll do laundry after you leave. And tomorrow? I have work. Where I will read emails and follow up with people and drink coffee and be this good little worker bee when, in reality, I want to peel my face off because I'm so bored."

"At least you're not dramatic about it," Essie replied.

"Ha, ha. All I'm saying is, you're telling me three men with hopefully large cocks are gonna put on masks and gloves, kidnap me and take me away from my life for a little while? I don't have to think, I don't have to talk, I don't have to make a single decision?" She stretched, catlike, in her chair. "Do you know how good I would sleep after getting fucked like that? Ugh, that alone makes it worth it."

The night ended shortly after that. As they were saying

goodbye to each other, their phones chirped in unison.

Kara Gibson had invited them to a barbeque. Tomorrow night.

"Let's ask her," Carly said. That interested gleam had returned to her eyes.

The close-knit suburb emerged from their dwellings with sacred, routine promptness. They assembled on sidewalks and began the short walk to Kara Gibson's, carrying round bowls full of potatoes, macaroni salad, and baked beans. The men carried twelve packs of beer, soda, and wine coolers.

Adorned in their ritualistic wear, they crossed the street in friendly salsa-colored sundresses or flowered skirts tied at the waist. The men all seemed to be bald, balding, or had so severely scalped their hair that it clung in neat, hedge-like lines along their skulls. They wore ball caps that were white and turned around backwards. Some had sunglasses; each had T-shirts and basketball shorts. They were each named something like Ryan, Dan, Tyler, or Bob. Their wives were an assortment of Chelsea's and Rachel's, with the occasional Mandy or Sandra.

Essie had a horrible sensation that any of them could be swapped with one another, and they wouldn't notice. *She* wouldn't notice; be it a Dan or a Ryan making clever observations for her benefit or criticizing the way Greg Gibson grilled.

The first barbeque she'd gotten dragged to, it felt

like the first day of a new school. Ryan had dragged her around, forcing her to meet the neighbors he already seemed to know.

Luckily she'd found Carly, a loud girl with colorful tattoos who was already a bit too drunk for 4 pm, who waved her over and asked why Essie looked so terrified.

"I'm not a people person," she admitted, and Carly replied that she was barely a person so... friends?

Everyone made their way to Kara Gibson's pool deck, Kara and Greg shaking hands and hugging people, the joyful chorus of Midwest greeting "Hey! Good to see ya!" shouted at one another, gleaming white teeth glinting in the Tiki Torch light.

Ryan disappeared from her side immediately and beelined for Ron and Jason at Greg's minibar.

Essie found Carly laying on a deck chair, watching the husbands in the pool as they tossed a football back and forth.

"They look like hot dogs," she said, tilting her chin at them.

The bald, tanned men wobbled back and forth in the water, like they were boiling.

"You've been smoking too much weed," Essie said.

"What?"

"You're calling people hot dogs."

"Not people, them! The bald ones in Kara's pool."

Carly's husband came over holding drinks. He handed one to Carly and one to Essie, saying, "Here, take mine. I want to make a stronger one anyway." Anderson was a lean, muscular man who seemed like he'd be more at ease fixing motorcycles than working in tech. He was shirtless, and Essie noticed a newer, blue-ink tattoo on the back of his hand. A small, sketched coffin. Carly was covered in them and had been pushing him to get tattoos for a while. It seemed like he was cracking.

"He brings me drinks and has his hair. I knew there was a reason I liked him," Carly said, kissing him then shoving him away. Anderson wandered off. The football soared out of the pool, and he caught and flipped it, grinning before disappearing back into the house.

"You two make me sick," Essie said.

Carly nodded. "Absolutely." Kara Gibson circled the pool while chatting with guests, handing a pink filled glass to someone in the pool. She paused to twirl in her sundress, showing it off for someone who asked. Carly watched her with wolf eyes, tracking her movements. "There she is. Want to go find out how to get kidnapped?"

Essie was watching Ryan talk a little too animatedly to their neighbor Lindsay, grinning too much and gesturing too freely. She recognized all the signs and signals; every blade of grass and green leaf pointed in that direction. Jealousy. She was supposed to feel jealous, right? But jealousy would mean she cared, and *cared* seemed like such a strong word.

The Kara Gibson mystery was much more interesting. Probably a trainwreck. Infidelity, a collapsing marriage, a messy divorce—all of it on the horizon for Kara. It was satisfying to pass the wreckage of someone else's life and examine it, curling your corrupt little soul around the idea that *oh, that'll never be me.*

Ryan laughed at something Lindsay said and reached out to briefly touch her hip.

Kara went into the house. Like bank robbers planning a heist, Carly and Essie glanced at each other.

They followed her into the house.

They cornered Kara in the kitchen, surrounding her on either end of the kitchen island and peering over a legion of martini glasses. Kara glanced from Essie to Carly, then back, folding her arms across her chest like she was a teenager in defiance of her parents.

"Hi! It is good to see you two!"

"Kara! You look so good in that dress," Carly replied, closing in.

"Your house looks great," Essie added, stepping forward.

Kara's friendly, placating smile dropped. Her penciled on eyebrows narrowed at Essie. "You told Carly?"

Essie shrugged.

"We didn't tell anyone else," Carly said. She leaned onto the counter. "But... what exactly are we keeping a secret?"

Essie had seen dogs in animal shelters, skittishly looking from human to human, backing itself deeper into its cage. Kara did that now, her eyes flicking back and forth. Essie wondered when her teeth would come out.

"I don't have to tell you anything," Kara said. "Maybe you should just leave."

"Maybe we should tell your husband—" Carly replied. Essie saw the flash of anger on Kara's face, the glint of meanness on Carly's, and slid smoothly between them.

Essie the mediator, the peacekeeper. "I just want to make sure you're alright. What I saw was... confusing," she said.

Kara frowned at her, then savored Carly with a glare. She plucked one of the martini glasses off the counter and sipped it, her lipstick leaving a faint pink mark on the glass. "It's a really, really good story," she said. "Hand me my purse." She pointed to it on the wall hook to Carly's left. Carly snagged it and tossed it to her. Kara unzipped the little black handbag and dug around in it before pulling out a metallic black card.

She slid it over the counter as Essie and Carly drew closer, peering down at it. The card was blank, save for a phone number engraved in it. Essie traced the numbers with the tip of her fingers as Kara began her story.

"I'm only telling *you* this," she said pointedly at Essie, "because I think you're going through something similar."

"What?"

"C'mon, I saw your husband with Lindsay. And you two don't exactly scream 'happy marriage'."

"Thanks, Kara," Essie replied dryly.

She shrugged. "Things with Greg haven't been good in a long time. Maybe years. But nobody wants to admit they're in a struggling marriage so I did what we all do. Post nice pictures on Facebook and go through the whole act like we're the exceptions. Everyone else falls apart, not Kara and Greg. Look how great we look on vacation." She said the last line with such bitterness that it made Essie want to cry.

"What happened? Anything specific or...?" Carly

asked.

"No... we just stopped touching each other. You know? Not even the sex but the shoulder bumps, the hugs, he used to put his forehead to mine and hold it there for a while—" Kara's face crumpled, and it seemed as if she were about to cry, but she recovered, rearranging her features back into suburban perfection. "We've been together for a long time. Maybe I'm boring. I don't know."

Carly gently reached out and touched her wrist. "So, the card?"

"Right! Sorry. So, things are getting worse and worse with Greg. Not even sleeping in the same bed. Basically roommates at this point. And I should just... talk to him. I should just reach out and say 'hey, something's wrong, can't you feel it?' but I don't."

She's living my life. Every word of it, Essie realized in a rush of joy at not being alone, followed by a swift torrent of despair because Kara's story didn't seem to have a happy ending.

"He's cheating," Carly remarked, as if she were commenting on the rain they were supposed to get.

Kara nodded. "Has been for a while. Some girl at work. She has an apartment in the city. I saw the texts."

Was Ryan getting those same texts? Was there some girl—some faceless, amorphous girl—innocent in her own way but still somehow vile?

Or maybe there wasn't someone else. Maybe whatever was happening between Essie and her husband was a deeper kind of broken. That felt worse somehow. Betrayal she could almost understand; the disintegration of something that had been good—once—was unbearable.

18

Kara gulped the last of her margarita. Essie hoped they weren't the first people she was telling about all this; that there was someone she could cry with, collapse against. A friend, a sister, a mother.

"I found out and I was going to confront him. Leave him, start the divorce. Everything. But..."

"You wanted revenge," Carly said, grinning.

"Yes. And I got it." She tipped her glass at the card. "Those men took care of me."

"So it's an escort service?" Essie asked.

"Nope. I didn't pay them anything."

Carly picked up the card. "Okay, enough dancing around. What happened?"

"Someone I went to school with had the card. It gets passed around from person to person. Very secretive. 'Give it to a girl in need,' sort of thing. I told this friend some of what was going on in my life and she slipped me this card." Kara smiled wanly. "I wouldn't have called it if Greg wasn't cheating. But one of the texts he sent to her, you know what it said?"

"What?" Carly asked.

"I can't wait to taste you." Kara was no longer looking at them. She was staring fixedly at her granite countertop, her eyes glassed over with rage-filled tears. "Can you believe that?" She took a deep breath. "I called the number on the card. I did everything they said. And I mean *everything.*"

"So you call—"

"You call and you'll get a voice on the phone. You agree to their terms and a group of men will kidnap you in a van and fuck you until you can't walk, Carly. Is that clear enough for you?"

Carly blinked and Essie laughed. "They're hookers?"

Kara shrugged. "The van is just for fun. They took me to a very nice penthouse. They even fed me breakfast. Maybe they're rich, bored lawyers with power fetishes. I don't know. I don't care. That's the whole point."

"You don't know their names?"

"I never saw their faces, Essie. Well, I saw one." She smiled dreamily. "He was my favorite."

"What about diseases or protection or... That's so fucking risky, did anyone know where you were?" Essie's chest tightened at the thought.

Kara smiled. "I'm not stupid. My friend had my location and knew where I was. As for the rest... Well, it wouldn't be fun if it wasn't a little risky."

A guest wandered in, asking Kara where the bathroom was. She pointed them in the right direction, and they wandered away. A silence fell between the women, before Kara spoke up.

"One of the... rules, I guess, is that I'm supposed to give someone else the card."

"Oh, it's like when people do the 'pay it forward' thing at the drive-thru, but for dick," Carly said dryly.

"So you don't want the card," Kara said.

"No, my marriage is fine, thanks."

She slid it to Essie, who held it in front of her like it was irradiated.

"Just in case," Kara said.

Someone outside called her name. Kara brushed past them, murmuring, "Excuse me." before slipping out to the pool deck.

Carly and Essie stood awkwardly in her kitchen. Essie slid the card into her pocket. Carly watched her and smirked. "Be careful, okay?"

"I'm not going to do it."

"Right. But be careful."

"Carly, I am not calling that number."

"Absolutely. You'd be insane to do something so risky and impulsive."

"Exactly."

"But be careful."

CHAPTER 3

Kara Gibson moved out of town hardly a week later.

Essie was turning her car onto her street, one of those vague work headaches jackhammering at her temples. When she got stressed, she wanted to sleep, but she knew for a fact that Ryan hadn't cooked anything, and the thought of fast food right now turned her stomach and the act of *going out* was just as bad.

When exactly did her life become jumping from the kiddie pool of stress and misery at work to diving into the deep end of stress and misery at home?

As she turned the car, a bright orange U-Haul lumbered

by, followed by a small black sedan. She recognized Kara, in full makeup, with a new haircut. Her backseat was stuffed with suitcases and boxes.

She was alone.

They glided past one another, locking eyes. Kara held her thumb and pinky to her ear, and for a split second, Essie thought she wanted Essie to call her.

Black card, Kara mouthed, and instantly it clicked.

And then, abruptly, Kara Gibson was gone.

Essie turned her own car into her own driveway, thinking about the black card.

She put the card inside of some old Christmas socks and forgot about it. Completely. Entirely. Absolutely.

Except not at all.

Every time Ryan breathed in a way she didn't like, she thought of the card.

When he closed his laptop too fast like he was hiding something, she thought about the dial tone ringing in her ear as she called those men.

On a miserable, failed date night, he ignored her to stare at his phone in the restaurant. She pictured black gloved hands encircling her neck. Tugging at her hair. Pulling down on her lips.

Essie had a loose code of things she did not do. When the marriage had been good, they were easy rules to follow. She swore not to be one of those snooping women; she gloated to girls at work about it. She didn't feel the need to sift through who her husband followed on social media. She didn't need his passcode for his phone. She was definitely, certainly not one of those women who needed constant reassurance. Her and Carly would make fun of women like that, the two of them drinking on her porch, assured that they, of all people, had mastered youthful, cool, enlightened modern marriage.

All of that was easy when Ryan brought flowers home every Friday. Or made breakfast on the weekends, wearing her purple apron and flipping pancakes. When they stayed awake watching movie after movie, or when they took long car rides together, going nowhere specific.

Then he withdrew, and the needy, panicky rat inside of Essie began to chew on the bars of its cage.

Until a mere few hours after Kara Gibson disappeared from her life, Essie was opening her husband's laptop, fingers fluttering over the keys, searching for some clue.

You're just looking for a reason to call the number on the card.

That insidious voice that sounded so much like Carly, telling her bitter, honest truths.

Ryan's browser history was clean.

His Facebook was bare. He kept around 60 friends, and the people he did message on there were all friends from high school; they talked about the latest video games coming out.

His Instagram featured pictures of his truck, a few pictures of them together on vacation. His bio simply said "play hard."

Did I marry the dullest man alive? Did they produce him in a factory?

A surreal sense of distance developed, where she got a glimpse at how others must see her husband and dismiss him as harmless. Insignificant.

The thoughts in her head were already bad, and they were quickly multiplying with sinister ease. A cheating spouse was one particular heartbreak.

A cheating spouse you weren't even sure you *liked* was an even more unique flavor of pain she didn't feel like examining.

Logging into his bank account would likely trigger a security alert. She could check his location—he assured her that he had gone to the gym—but that was crazy wife territory.

I'm not that far gone.

His laptop let out a cheery whistle, letting her know that a new email had just dropped in his inbox.

He'd left that logged in.

I'm the chill wife. I don't nag. I don't snoop. I'm cool.

She clicked the icon and the page opened before her.

Thanks for checking in at Covington Inn, the computer said.

Here is your confirmation number.

Enjoy your stay!

Enjoy fucking someone else in our clean bed! Enjoy her body on top of yours underneath cool, crisp sheets!

Essie closed her eyes and saw the conversation play out. Confronting him. His dismissive shrug when he tried to make it seem like she was making a big deal out of nothing.

Then the lie.

"I just go there to get some sleep. I have a hard time

sleeping in our bed."

"I need some space."

"I'm not cheating."

"I would never, ever, do that to *you*, Essie. Sweet, gorgeous Essie. Love of my life. We have a house together. We have almost a decade of love. How could you think that of *me*?"

Or maybe he wouldn't. Maybe he'd shrug and say, "Yeah, you caught me. Let's get lawyers."

No fighting.

Banal acceptance.

The thought of it drove a savage wedge of anger between her eyes, tears welling up and spilling down her cheeks.

She wanted to burn down the fucking house.

Instead, she found the black card.

And dialed the number.

Ryan said nothing as she bustled around the following day. She felt his eyes on her as she spent much of the morning looking into the bathroom mirror; applying makeup, wiping it off, reapplying it. She applied eyeliner like she was performing brain surgery; scalpel precision, steady hands, steady.

She went through three outfits, rejected them, tried them each again, rejected two of them, dug in her closet for a dress that didn't fit right anymore, almost gave up entirely, and went back in the closet.

On the phone, Essie had been greeted by a firm, almost bored sounding receptionist. A woman. Essie stammered out that she'd received the card from a friend and was just curious what it was all about.

The woman on the other end cut her off. "This line is for setting up a meeting with Woods. Would you like to set a meeting?"

"Woods? Is that one of their names?"

"Yes. Would you like to set a meeting?"

"Um..."

"He has tomorrow at 2 pm available. Public setting. He will discuss details."

"Hold on, I don't—"

"Yes, you do. You called this number for a reason. Your name?"

"Essie."

"Okay, Essie. You will receive a text message with a location. For all intents and purposes, this is like a job interview. Woods will meet with you for about twenty minutes and will decide if he wants to move forward." The woman paused, and Essie heard furious typing. "You can back out at any time before, after, or during the meeting. Safety and consent are priorities for us."

Essie laughed. "You guys sound like my cable company."

The receptionist clucked her tongue. "2 pm. Does that work for you?"

"Yeah, I guess."

Essie received a text with a location, and was amused to find it was a small, locally owned coffee shop. She'd been expecting official looking envelopes and black cars, billionaires buying women for pleasure. Silk and suits, meticulously groomed men who were cut from an Armani ad. She pictured glittering wrist watches that cost more than her life and bedsheets from some far off oppressed land, like all that suffering made them softer.

How do you dress for something like this? Half job interview, half "are you going to fuck me" tryout? Do I wear business casual? A dress? If I dress slutty, will I be taken seriously? If I dress formally, will I not seem into it?

Even more enticing was that these fresh, new anxieties absorbed her, and she was able to avoid giving a single new thought to Ryan, who watched her dress and undress over and over again.

Finally, he asked, "Are you going somewhere?"

The excuse was ready-made and it really didn't fucking matter if he believed her. "Out with some friends. Shouldn't be gone long."

A flicker of excitement crossed his face, but he stifled it. "Okay. Be safe."

He's going to message his other woman.

She gazed at him, wondering if this was the moment where she revealed that she knew. They would fight, and maybe they would reconcile and fix things. They'd be that mature, serene couple who'd "gone through things" and come out stronger.

No.

No.

Fuck. That.

She picked out a flowery sundress that clung to her nicely and slipped it on. She gave up on her hair, which seemed bent on being frizzy and chaotic. On her way out the door, she paused and kissed Ryan, shoving her tongue into his mouth with so much force and eagerness that his eyes widened and he laughed.

"Wow, you haven't kissed me like that in a while."

I'm going to do the same exact thing to another man's cock.

The thought gave her power, enough so that she was able to give him a genuine smile before grabbing her purse and leaving the house.

She drove down the same road she'd seen Kara Gibson on. She wondered if Kara had the same knot of anxiety in her stomach. If she had the same flickering doubt, the urge to turn the car around and stay safe, routine, and miserable.

But had Kara Gibson been this fucking turned on?

CHAPTER 4

Essie got an outside table at the coffee shop, double checked the pepper spray in her bag, and tried to relax. Around her, cars zipped by, people pushed children in strollers, a jackhammer rattled somewhere in the distance. The normalcy of it all seemed to mock her.

She was aware of a certain self-destructive streak in her. One of those defects that therapy and repeated mistakes were eager to point out. But all that had done was made her frustratingly aware of it. She'd become a second guesser, an "I don't know" type of person, and she resented that. She'd done well in school, just to flunk out of boredom and depression in her sophomore year of college. Her relationship before Ryan imploded, which let's face it, was her fault. A few failed careers before landing on Ryan, who seemed like a warm, safe beach after being caught in vicious undertow and taken to deep waters.

Now that was falling apart, but at least this time it wasn't her fault.

Right?

The panicky rat chewed on her ribcage again.

I don't care I don't care I don't care how I feel, I am doing this I am tired of this, this person I've become, so needy and desperate and unsure I HATE IT

Essie remembered the steely glint in Kara Gibson's eyes after her experience with the men in the van. The way she'd simply left, chin stuck forward, cutting apart her life with cold, calculated precision.

Essie wanted that.

Needed it.

A man approached the table and her excitement sputtered. He was broad shouldered, sure, but his eyebrows had a caveman, unkempt look and his facial hair was patchy and reminded her of an aggressive moss growing up the side of a tree. The man walked directly toward her table, looked over at her, smiled...

And then walked by.

Essie checked her phone. 2:07. The waitress came along, forcing her to order another coffee.

By 2:15 she was ready to leave. The plan was to go cry on Carly's couch. Let Carly fill her head with that best friend confidence and then maybe she could go home and deal with it.

A tall, slender man with brown, almost blonde hair that was cut short, passed by her table. He was wearing a red T-shirt and slim fitting jeans that clung tightly to his hips. She watched the muscles in his back move against the shirt as he looked around, confused, the sharp cut of his jaw catching the sun. He looked like he'd be at home in a cowboy movie, sauntering through town to get into a gunfight at the saloon.

He turned around, his thin, slightly lined face puzzled, before spotting her and smiling. He took two steps, paused, scratched his head, pulled out his phone, glanced at it, then looked back at her. "Are you Essie?"

"Yes, that's me."

"I'm Woods."

He grinned, extending a hand. She shook it, feeling calluses and rough skin. His arm hair was long and turned blonde in the sunlight. It was easy to imagine him fixing something on her car, his hands smudged with black oil. Or on his back in her kitchen, his head tucked (*under her skirt*) under the sink wrenches and ratchets and whatever else spread out beside him, his hips shifting in his jeans as he tried to reach a particular bolt.

"I'm so late, I'm sorry. Let me get a coffee and then we'll talk?" He let go of her hand and went into the coffee shop, only to reappear a moment later with a foam cup. He sat down and began rubbing his eyes, yawning. "I'm having one of those days. Set my keys down, couldn't remember where I put them. Found them, picked 'em up, and got to my truck. Know what I did? Forgot my wallet. I go back to the house. Find my wallet. Get back to my truck. Wait,

35

where did my keys go? I left them back in the house." He brought the cup to his lips, his gentle green eyes shifting upward to search her face. "I don't think I'm very good at being alive."

His last words stood out to her, and struck her as an awkward, but sincere offering. It wasn't rare to meet people who seemed to spill forth and give you huge chunks of their lives in a bid to get to know you. But normally they were women, or older people, eager to connect with someone. You caught them in grocery lines or waiting rooms, and suddenly you were ten minutes into a conversation you didn't want to have, learning every detail about a nice, oblivious old woman's cats.

Men, especially attractive men like Woods, only seemed to act like that when they wanted to manipulate you. *Here's my vulnerabilities, Essie. Here's how real and honest I am, how down to earth. I'm different, I see through the bullshit.*

Her defenses sprang into action. A thousand spears in her mind formed lines, rows of shields assembled, and a legion of arrows were pulled back and aimed at Woods.

It's not a date, though.

You called him. He didn't know you existed.

Essie gave him a diplomatic smile. "I don't think I'm very good at being alive either."

"It's a nightmare, for sure. So—" He stretched, his shoulder joints popping loudly. "I'm sure you have questions. I have things to go over. Details, details, details. You got our card from a friend, and she gave you some story, and it's something you want to try."

She frowned. "It's something I'm considering."

"Right, right. You're possibly, maybe, perhaps

considering asking three men to kidnap and fuck your brains out." He nodded vigorously, sipping the coffee again, like he was pantomiming a lawyer who had just heard an expected argument.

"Can you keep your voice down?"

He ignored her. He got to his feet and tossed some money down onto the table. "Get up," he said.

"What?"

Woods sighed. "I can't do this if it feels like a bad date. And right now it's less of a date and more of a... job interview. Which could be a fun roleplay 'how bad do you want this job' type deal, but like..." He gestured at the sidewalk. "What if we walk and you tell me why you're interested, and I'll explain how we do our best to make it safe and enjoyable for everyone." He held out his hand, bowing slightly. She didn't think it was intentional, but for a second, he seemed like a fancy British aristocrat, asking for her courtship.

This man, who, by all accounts was some sort of sex freak, was being more gentlemanly and... fucking *romantic* than the man who'd looked her in the eyes and lied through his wedding vows.

She took his hand and let herself be pulled upright. They began walking together, Woods letting go of her hand very quickly. He walked with his hands around his coffee, twiddling his fingers against the black lid, but sometimes their shoulders would brush. He made no move to put any distance between them.

Neither did Essie.

"You're not what I expected," she told him. A man on a bicycle split between them. They rejoined side by side as

Woods answered.

"Well, look at it from my point of view. You're a woman, meeting a strange guy for something that is... dangerous. It wouldn't be enticing if it wasn't, but let's face it: you're taking a risk." His eyes took an interest in one of the shops they were passing, and they lingered in front of it as he examined a collection of miniature lighthouses behind a glass window. "I have to convince a woman to trust me enough to throw her in a van and do all sorts of filthy, disgusting, wonderful things to her." They moved on, their walk slowing as two women pushing strollers took up the entire sidewalk. He slowed his pace and Essie matched it, another flicker of attraction tickling at her brain.

It was so easy to walk with him. She was always walking so much faster than people. Ryan, obviously, but even Carly and her best friends from back home. But Woods' body language and steady, fluid stride let her use her quick, furious steps as she filled the gap to keep up. Something about the angle of his shoulders told her when to slow down, when to separate or walk in front as they maneuvered around people, him keeping her on the right, away from the trash cans and road.

"Anyway," he said, "the only way to do it is to be direct and kind of... I don't know, relaxed about it?"

"You do seem very relaxed."

"Thank you. I'm actually quite nervous."

"Yeah?"

"Yeah. So that's the first thing. I'm the face of the group. I'm the guy in charge of making sure things don't go too far." He pointed at a security camera, perched like a shiny black beetle on the streetlight. "You've been seen in public with me. At the end of this, if anything happens to you, I'm the first suspect people will look for."

"That's... smart. Do you run into problems? From women, I mean?"

Woods shook his head. "Not really. Once in a while someone will want a relationship with one of the guys. But they don't take off their masks."

"Do you?" Essie asked, hoping he did.

"Yeah. The mask and gloves thing is cool for a while but it gets very warm and—" He nudged her. "—I like to talk a lot."

"Oh! Right." She blanched, unsure how to take any of this. Why was she here? How? This was the closest thing to a first date she'd been on in almost six years, and this guy belong to some... orgy cult, so obviously he was at least a little fucked in the head. And yet!

Butterflies. That little flicker of attraction.

I might actually do this.

Woods drained the rest of his coffee and pitched it in a trash can as they walked. The sun glowed on them with pleasant warmth, and a high, cool breeze brought fresh, faintly sea-smelling air to them, knocking away the car fumes and dingy smell of the city. She could smell him, too. Softer than cologne. Comfortable and clean. Laundry soap, like his clothes had just gotten out of the dryer.

Maybe it was all imagination; Essie trying to convince herself things were good in an attempt to avoid accepting how unraveled and strange her life was becoming.

Or maybe this guy was giving her good feelings when she'd been in a knot of misery and anxiety for weeks.

"So... how does it work?" she asked. "Do I meet the other guys?"

"Nope. You won't meet Owen and Levi. They prefer to stay anonymous. Keep in mind that this isn't just for you, there are other people involved with their own limits and boundaries."

"No, I didn't mean that, I just... Really?"

Woods placed a hand gently on her shoulder and steered her away from a group of tables set out in front of a restaurant. She'd been too busy looking at him and talking that she'd nearly crashed into them.

"Men have fantasies, too," he remarked. "But it can get complicated."

They were two strangers, Essie marveled. Two complete strangers having an intimate discussion about sex. "Complicated how?"

They rounded the corner of the block. "We pretend like emotions don't get caught up in sex," Woods said. "But they do. It's hard to get around. If I have a girlfriend, or a wife, and I love her very much, and there's a deep connection... I'm not going to share her with other men. That would destroy me. But..." He sipped the coffee. "A woman you don't know? A mutual fling? Something with a little roleplay? There's enough emotional distance for it to be good for everyone."

"I get that, but why the black card thing?"

"A fantasy is a fantasy, Essie. Some things are just really, really fun. So..." He mimicked pulling a mask on. "Masks, gloves, anonymity. They play a character, get into it, they're not responsible for the emotions afterward." He grinned at her. She could imagine him grinning the same way as she took off his clothes in front of him—hungry, lustful. "We get what we want, you get what you want."

They rounded the next corner, turning back towards the coffee shop again. They would be back there shortly, and she would have to decide. She didn't want to decide. She just wanted to keep walking and talking with this man.

"Can you explain to me how exactly this would happen? I'm not saying yes, I just want to hear a... I don't know."

He laughed. "You want to hear what a 'regular day on the job' looks like? You really want this to be a job interview, huh? Alright, let's see if you hire me." He cleared his throat. "So, you'll pick a date and time. Most women pick nighttime. You tell us where you will be, and we'll come pick you up."

"Pick up?"

His voice downshifted, becoming low and stern. "We throw a hood on you, zip-tie your hands and feet together, and put you in the van."

Oh God, why was that hot? "And then what?"

"We rent a hotel suite." He looked around. "Yeah, it's not too far from here. A hundred bucks to the desk guy, he lets us use the maintenance elevator. We carry you in, take you to the room and... Well, I won't spoil the surprise." His gaze pivoted from down the street to her. His eyes dragged down her body and then lifted back to her eyes. "Come on, Essie. You know exactly what will happen."

I do. I'm not admitting it but I think I've already decided.

They ambled leisurely back to the coffee shop. She

41

could see their table, still empty. They walked in amiable silence. Like they were coming from a pleasant brunch.

"How'd I do?" he asked suddenly.

"What?"

"All this," he said, "this was better right? Much better than arriving in a limo or something and throwing a sex contract on a table, right? I can never decide if these things should be official and professional, or relaxed and approachable."

"If you'd shown up in a suit with a briefcase, I would've thought I was getting taken by human traffickers."

He did a fist pump, a boyish, innocent smile breaking across his face. "Yes! Cool! Good! I worry about it so much, this is the worst part. It's so fucking awkward, but Levi is huge and that would freak people out. Owen is new and still shy about things so it's on me."

She'd forgotten about the other men. Their names hit the pool of emotions and caused ripples. Were the others like him at all? What would they think of her? "You'll be there, right?" she asked. "You said you were there to make sure things didn't go too far, does that mean you just, uh, watch?"

They were very close to the coffee shop now. She could see the dollar bills Wood's had left on their table fluttering slightly in the wind.

Woods stopped her, catching her wrist lightly. He tilted her chin up to him and gazed coldly at her. The mirth faded from him so rapidly that it was frightening.

Her heart clenched and a pit of nervousness began working in her stomach. But she knew it was a test. He was seeing if she was a curious tourist getting an easy thrill or if she was actually going to follow through.

"Oh, I'm going to fuck you, Essie." His face grew stern. "I'm going to do things to you that you'll be thinking about every time you touch yourself for the rest of your life." He let go and began walking away. She hurried to keep up. The coldness left him immediately. "Someone has to be the responsible one, though," he said jovially.

They were at their table.

"That's it," he said. "That's the whole pitch. If it sounds like something you want to try, you'll get a text with a form to fill out. Safe words, stuff you want to do, don't want to do, who to contact if there's an emergency." Now he sounded like a sales rep; like he was about to ask if she wanted the extended warranty.

"Wow, that's really organized."

He shrugged. "We operate on word of mouth, so we try to make sure things are pleasant for everyone."

"And if I say I don't want to do this?"

Woods smiled. "Then I ask that you give the card back. We only have a few."

Had he said all this to Kara Gibson? Was he the same man around her? Was this chemistry something he was able to conjure for every woman, like some sort of deadly flower luring her in?

You called him. You're worried his ulterior motive is sex? Isn't that why you're here? It's simple. Do you want to fuck him, Essie?

Yes.

God, yes.

Essie held her phone out awkwardly, like she was waiting for it to ring. She let out a high, shrill laugh. "I guess I'll wait for that text then!" She said it too loud, her laugh forced. Vaguely, she hoped a car would careen off the road and take out the entire cafe, ending this whole nervous nightmare.

Woods gave her a bemused grin. "Okay," he said. "Make sure you fill everything out. I'll see you soon." He shook her hand, laughing again. "I never know if we're supposed to hug or kiss or whatever after this part, it's so weird. Bye!" He turned abruptly away. Essie remembered what he'd said about being nervous, too.

She watched him walk away. Just before he turned the corner, he stopped and patted the pockets of his jeans.

He was making sure he hadn't forgotten his keys.

CHAPTER 5

By the time she got home, she'd talked herself out of it. Completely, entirely. She wasn't thinking clearly; she was making decisions based around emotions. Very strong emotions that made her want to scream-cry at the stoplight. Her impulsive, vindictive streak wanted to get out, wanted to go for a run, but it was fine. She had it leashed.

She drove down her street. Under control. What a normal thing.

She stopped for a group of kids circling on bikes. They waved to her, and she waved back. Routine. She'd done that a thousand times. She could just keep doing that a thousand more times.

She parked the car. How many more times would she do that in her normal, routine life? Countless, certainly.

Ryan was on the porch, checking the little black mailbox. Essie would get out, kiss him on the cheek, tickle his side, and ask what he wanted to do about dinner.

As she stepped out of the car, a young woman jogged by, hair bouncing in a ponytail. She wore one of those stretchy grey exercise outfits. She had headphones jammed into her ears and was staring straight ahead as she ran, her eyes meeting Essie's with a brief nod in her direction before lowering her head and running a little faster past them.

Essie looked up to see Ryan watching the woman as she ran away from them.

Their eyes met too, briefly, and he went back inside the house.

How would he feel knowing Woods looked at me like that?

The thought was heated and vicious. And she liked feeling vicious a lot more than mourning her marriage.

At work that Friday she received a text with a link. It was a simple document that outlined that she was a consenting adult, understood the risks, etc. She read it at her desk, ignoring the occasional *ding* from her computer as emails came in.

The form requested that she have an emergency contact.

That was easy. Carly.

She'd have to face Carly and get through her smirking and saying, "I told you so," but that was fine. For once, Essie was going to be the interesting one. She loved Carly to death but sometimes, *sometimes* her best friend's constant desire to be the cool, aloof older sister to her got on Essie's nerves. Carly was so wise, so cynical...

But she hadn't done this.

Below is a list of kinks/scenarios. Check yes on those you are comfortable with, or interested in trying.

Choking
Spanking
Degradation
Use of toys (dildos, vibrators, wands...)
Whips
Bondage
Marking

She scrolled down the list, eyes widening at the possibilities, trying to imagine each one.

Trying to imagine Woods doing all of them to her.

Essie checked a few, but at the bottom she noticed a special one:

Black Card's Choice: We'll do whatever the fuck we want to you.

Somewhere in the office behind her, a coworker asked if they were getting new monitors. Outside, a train whistled. Another email dinged on her desktop.

There was a possibility that this was going to be the most exciting thing she'd ever done.

And she didn't want Woods to think of her as vanilla and boring. Maybe that was how Ryan saw her; maybe that was how she'd gotten into this in the first place.

She checked Black Card's Choice with her thumb and sent it back to them.

Then she pretended to focus on her work. She answered two emails and made copies. She was fine, utterly fine, until her phone rang.

It was Woods.

"We'll take you tonight," he said. "9 pm. Text us an address."

He hung up before she could respond.

Essie left work early, telling her boss she didn't feel well. That was, at least in part, the truth. Her stomach was doing backflips and she'd chewed the nails on her left hand to bare nubs.

Carly, at least, didn't laugh.

They stood briefly on Carly's front porch; Essie told her everything very quickly, eager to be off and away in case Carly wanted to talk her out of it.

She didn't. "Be careful. Send me the address of the hotel before you leave. You have that, right?"

"Yes."

"Keep your phone on. I will call to check in. Otherwise—" Carly sparked up a cigarette and looked behind her to make sure her husband wasn't listening. "Get fucked, Essie."

"I... will do my best," she replied.

"I'm proud of you," Carly said suddenly.

"What?"

"Proud of you. Ya know, not taking shit laying down. Getting revenge." She blew smoke. "Pretty badass."

"Just trying to be like you," Essie said. They hugged briefly. Carly was not overly fond of displays of affection, but this was a rare exception.

It was really happening.

Ryan didn't notice that his wife shaved her legs or spent hours in the bathtub. He didn't notice the moisturizer lathered onto her elbows and shins, as if the Black Card Men would suddenly decide a dry elbow would make her unfuckable.

He sat at his computer, ignorant to the eyeshadow, the lip gloss, the studded earrings and the careful, primly pinned-back hairstyle. She strode past him in a thin white tank top and tiny gray shorts that clung to her in a way that made her slightly embarrassed.

If he smelled the perfume when she hugged him, he didn't mention it. He did see the bag slung over her shoulder, though. "Are you going somewhere?"

Essie nodded. "Yeah, I'm going to go stay with Carly. It's her birthday."

(It wasn't.)

"I forgot. How long will you be gone?"

"I'll be back Saturday evening."

That look of greed washed over his face; he didn't even try to hide it. "Okay, okay yeah. Sounds good. I might..."

He jerked his thumb back at the computer, and for a second, she wondered if he was going to accidentally tell the truth. "I might see what one of my friends is doing."

"Have fun," Essie replied, deciding to beg Woods to cum in her mouth.

Whatever there had been with her husband was dead. There was only the hurting left.

Well, and revenge.

Revenge could come first.

Smart, sensible women like Essie weren't supposed to dress like this.

They weren't supposed to walk alone at night wearing shorts that barely covered her.

They weren't supposed to meet hot men for anonymous sex.

In fact, women weren't supposed to want sex at all. It was *supposed* to be love. She could hear every bit of advice, warning, reproach, and guidance she'd received over the course of her entire life, yearning to stop her from doing this.

But she'd done as she had been told. She met someone, married him, and set her sights on gentle, wholesome, tender lovemaking. That was respectable. It was honest. She didn't go out to clubs and she didn't flirt with anyone. She had severed any notions of risky, exhilarating sexuality to fit her role as loving wife.

And he cheated on her.

She heard the van rumbling down the road and suppressed a smile. She refused to turn around and face it, even as the headlights flooded the area around her, illuminating the sidewalk and bathing the trimmed hedges in white light.

The brakes squeaked but she didn't turn around.

The van door slid open, grinding on its tracks. She kept walking. Her heart was beating very fast. Soon, she'd feel their hands. Would they be rough? Would they warn her first? Would they ask for her ID to make sure? Or would they just take her, slap her across the face and tell her to get fucking ready for it, you belong to us now Essie.

Footsteps behind her. She walked a little quicker—*why is it so hot to be chased?*—before breaking into a run.

"Oh no you don't," one of them said.

And then they were on her. Black gloved hands, white hockey masks that made their breath heavy and muffled as the two men grabbed her. One around her hips, the other capturing her with massive arms around her shoulders.

"Hold her still," the other grunted. He had a roll of tape and quickly bound her wrists behind her back. Her legs were next, and then, with breathtaking ease, she was tossed over the large man's shoulder and carried to the open door.

This is it, this is real, I've been fucking kidnapped, oh my God.

Inside the van, she was laid across their laps. The van had been fitted with a bench seat that ran parallel to the walls, like a limousine. She caught a glimpse of it as the bag was torn off, before her head was shoved down into the thighs of one the men. A gloved hand pulled her hair back and made her turn to look into the dark void of the masked man's eyes. He had a massive, powerful chest; it strained against the black T-shirt he was wearing. His hand seemed to engulf her entire face as it clamped around her jawline, a gloved thumb hooking against her lower lip. His other hand dug into the front of his pants and pulled out his cock; it curved upward and seemed ridiculously hard already.

The other man who had captured her bent her over his lap, a hand squeezing her ass while the other draped over the small of her back, holding her firmly in place.

She could hear their breath, panting behind the masks. She could smell hints of their colognes and body washes, citruses and cedar scents. Faintly, there was the smell of fresh linen, like clothes that just got out of the wash. *Woods.*

She remembered how he smelled, and that's only something she did when she had a crush—

There wasn't time to think. If there was, she'd have backed out. This was insane; every sense of self-preservation told her this was a bad idea.

But a dick was already in her mouth.

"It's good to see you, Essie," Woods said from the driver's seat. "You've met Owen and Levi. You have Levi's dick in your mouth right now. Essie, do me a favor and say, 'Hello, Levi.'"

Levi held her still, his dick forcing its way past the back of her teeth, hitting her throat. For a brief, struggling second she couldn't breathe. Then he began bobbing her head up and down, like an obedient toy. He pulled her up, his masked face tilting as he examined the saliva dripping down her chin.

"Hello, Le—"

Her words were silenced by his cock, both hands on the back of her head, his hips thrusting upward in steady, rhythmic fashion.

"We can't hear you, Essie," Woods called out. "Try again, sweetheart."

A stinging slap sent pain radiating on her ass. Owen spanked her again, making her cry out against Levi, the vibration of her voice making him groan, and *that* sent pleasure coursing through Essie.

She hadn't had a single, coherent thought other than her mouth, Levi's cock, and Owen's hands as they rubbed her pussy over the crotch of her shorts. Levi got harder and harder in her mouth.

So much power in simply being wanted.

If she had time to think, she'd almost feel pathetic.

But Owen ripped the shorts down and she felt the latex tracing the outline of her labia, circling her entire pussy, squeezing the hood of her clit between his forefingers before letting go and moving in a firm, eager circle.

Then it was all interrupted by another sharp spank, this one higher up on her ass, and she could feel the radiating imprint of Owen's entire hand.

She yelped, and out of the corner of one blurry eye, saw Levi tilt his head upward in ecstasy.

"Hello, Levi," she said around his cock. It came out muffled and wet, but the friction of her teeth grazing him was almost too much for him to handle, because his hands tightened around her head and he slammed his cock to the hilt. He held her there for an entire second before releasing her—gasping, fresh spit coating his thighs, tears streaking her mascara.

"Do that again," Levi said. His voice was surprisingly soft and quiet, as if he were a man who didn't need to talk much. The way his arms bulged against his T-shirt, and the way the cords stood out in his neck, Essie assumed he probably didn't need to.

Essie was discovering a new aspect of herself; a thirst to prove herself. To show that she could keep up with these men. She wasn't going to be a mewling housewife who came twice and fell asleep. She wanted to see them moan; to fall apart with what she could do to them, to get jealous of each other when she devoted all her attention to one of them.

She rolled slightly onto her right shoulder, Levi steadying her on his giant knees. "Untie me and I might," she said sweetly.

Quietly, from the front seat, with great sincerity and a touch of malice, Woods said, "You don't make the rules, Essie. We do."

Owen slid his finger entirely inside of her and began pumping it in and out, pausing after every four or so thrusts to tease her asshole with his thumb.

Levi took back control of her mouth, this time slapping her face lightly with his hand, the head of his cock stuffed into the side of her check. "Say hello again," he demanded.

"Hello—" She gasped. "Levi."

"Good girl. I like it when you use a little teeth."

The van hit a bump and he slipped out of her mouth, the shaft bouncing against her lips. He took the opportunity to guide her to his balls, where she began licking and sucking, pulling on the flesh with her mouth, using her teeth to drag lightly against his skin.

By his gasps and the way his fingers were digging into her, Levi was enjoying her.

"I might keep you right here for the rest of the ride," he remarked. "This mouth, right here."

She tried again to get him to break. "Really? I thought you'd be fucking me by now."

Woods hit the brakes—hard—the entire van coming to a jolting halt. Everyone in the back slid forward, Levi reaching and failing to grab the driver's seat headrest. Owen slid to the ground, his shoulders slamming into Levi's ribs, sending them both into a tangled heap against the back of Woods' seat.

Essie, bound and helpless, was flung from their laps and landed with a thud on the hard rubber-matted floor. She landed on her stomach, the wind knocked out of her.

"Sorry," Woods said cheerfully. "Thought I could beat the red." She had fallen close to the open space between the front two seats. Her chin rested near the gearshift in the floor. Woods had one wrist hanging loosely over the steering wheel, the other hand absentmindedly caressing the knob of the shifter. The other guys were busy untangling themselves and adjusting their masks.

"Are you okay?" Woods asked, looking under his right arm like she was a cup in his cup holder. His mask was smaller than the others. They all wore the white masks, but his clung to the angles in his face, the eyeholes clear, revealing his glittering green gaze. It gave him a pensive, owlish appearance.

She grunted. "I didn't check the box for 'car accident.'"

The mask shifted. She could tell he was smiling. "You didn't say you were going to be a brat either. Or dress that fucking slutty."

"Can't a girl dress like she's asking for it?"

"Sweetheart, you were begging for it in those shorts. Did your husband plead with you not to leave in them?"

The words struck her like a slap in the face. The emotional turmoil was close to the surface, no matter how much adrenaline and sexual excitement she tried to hide in.

Woods observed her. He reached down to stroke her hair. "We'll take care of you Essie. Don't worry." He reached up and adjusted his rearview mirror. "Levi?"

"Yeah?"

"We have about five minutes until we're at our destination. Do you think you can fill our slut with cum by that time?"

Levi answered by climbing onto her, pinning the back of her thighs against his meaty legs. A viselike hand clamped down on her shoulder while she felt latex fingers spreading her pussy open and guiding his cock in.

She gasped. Woods' hand snatched her ponytail and arced her neck so she was looking upward. "I like that noise," he said quietly. "I love hearing you take it." He kept one hand on the steering wheel, one on her as she laid trapped between the front seats.

Levi began pounding her, his hips slamming against her ass, the rubber flooring pulling at the skin on her stomach. Her shoulders ached from the restraints; she had a bruise she could feel forming on her knee. Spit and sweat coated her neck.

It felt so good being dirty.

Being used.

The first orgasm wasn't even one of pleasure; it was escapism, excitement—the fact that her life suddenly felt different, like she was erasing a whiteboard and feeling the satisfaction of the dark marks fading with each pass of the eraser.

Levi grunted in her ear. Told her how tight she was. How sexy she was. How he wanted to spank her ass and cum in her mouth. How much she turned him on.

Woods held her up for the rest of the drive—looking down to watch her moan, gazing at her half-closed eyes.

At one of the stoplights, he began rubbing the front of his jeans while he looked at her.

She had time to wonder what his cock looked like when Levi climbed off her and told Owen to take a turn.

Woods laughed and said he'd take the scenic route.

CHAPTER 6

When the van finally rumbled to a stop, Owen and Levi were passing her back and forth—taking turns using her mouth, their hands exploring her body, squeezing her thighs, caressing her breasts. Every nerve on her body ached with anticipation.

The van door snapped open. Woods gestured for the men to release her. The bag was thrown back over her head, shrouding her in darkness. The shorts were pulled back onto her and she was guided out of the van. She heard something click. One of them leaned down and cut the zip ties around her ankles.

Woods was in her ear. He grabbed the back of her neck, pinching the pressure points. She curled against him in both pleasure and discomfort. "Walk," he hissed. "Do not make a sound."

She was shoved blindly forward. The experience dissolved into muffled blackness as she strained to see through the cloth. She listened and tried to piece together the sounds around her. Van doors closing. Their footsteps, harsh on pavement. A parking garage?

"One step up, right here. Lift your legs," Wood ordered. "Good. Keep walking."

A door hinge squealed. Her foot caught on something, and she stumbled. Multiple pairs of hands caught her, lifted her off the ground slightly, and reset her.

"Sorry," Woods muttered, momentarily breaking character. "There was a rug in the doorway."

Something dinged, and there was the sound of rattling. An elevator. They stood still, Essie turning her head back and forth, trying to get a sense of where she was.

"Do you think anyone saw us?" a new voice said. Stiff, monotone. Familiar in a way that was hard to place. Was that Owen? He hadn't spoken yet, even as he and Levi took turns on her in the van.

"Doorman might have," Woods replied. "That's why we're taking the maintenance elevator."

"Will it be a problem?"

"No, I don't think so. Besides..." Woods' breath was suddenly on her neck. Was that his chest pressing against her shoulder? Okay, and yep, those were his hands, sliding down the front of her shorts, stroking her pussy with confident ease.

Like he owned her.

Her knees buckled and she bit back a moan. She didn't want to give him the satisfaction of knowing how turned on he made her.

"If someone asks, we'll show them the disclaimer Essie signed. All the things we're allowed to do to her. Everything she *wants* us to do." He punctuated the word *wants* with a squeeze of her sensitive, swollen clit, firing an electrode into her brain, and she let out a yelp.

The elevator dinged again. She heard doors parting open. Essie was shoved into the elevator, hitting the back of it and bouncing off. She felt the floor shift under their weight as each man climbed in after her.

The doors closed. The elevator began to rumble.

"It moves slow," Levi remarked.

"I'm sure we can figure out something to do," Woods replied.

There was a long enough pause for her to shift her weight from one heel to another, sweeping her blinded gaze around, wondering what direction the next stimuli would come from.

Zzzzt.

Zzzzt.

Zippers undone.

Someone's chin perched itself on her shoulder. Their jaw jutted against her skin as they spoke. Woods—of course it was Woods. Essie wondered if he was ever going to fuck her, or if this whole thing was simply a sick power fantasy for him.

"I'm going to untie you," he said. "I want you to keep your hands by your sides. Can you do that for me?"

"I guess."

"Essie?"

"What?"

"If you say 'yes sir' I'll fuck you right here in the elevator. Do you want that?"

Things were escalating. The distant shore of her life with Ryan was fading as this roaring current of new sensation and depravity dragged her further and further out.

Her thoughts spasmed in short, frantic bursts, caught between racing, anxiety-riddled thoughts screaming at her to end this now; get back to Ryan, to her house, put on her sweatpants, curl up and be safe, secure, and boring. This was too much—these men, their van, the masks, the domination. She couldn't imagine what they were going to do to her—

Yes you can, her mind whispered. These were the other thoughts. The voice of lust and disdain for who she'd become. *You know exactly what they're going to do to you. And you want it. You're just pretending not to because you think you're supposed to. That there's some rule saying you can't do this. No one's judging you, Essie. You want this man to fuck you, so tell him.*

In her left hand, and her right, she felt something slide against her palm. She willingly wrapped her fingers around each cock and began stroking. On her left, Levi. She recognized the curve. On the right, Owen—thicker, uncircumcised—

Oh God. I'm remembering their dicks.

Woods' began choking her lightly, his palm pressing against her throat. "Say it," he growled in her ear.

This is what you called them for, Essie.

"Yes, sir," she gasped. "I want you to fuck me."

The bag was ripped off her head, revealing a dimly lit elevator. The men were grouped around her, the masks passive but pulsing as they breathed heavily. The elevator had a marker for which floor they were on, and it caught her eye in a distant, abstract sort of way. Floor 3 of 22.

Woods held her still as he undid his belt. Without having to tell them, the other men hooked their fingers around the waistband of her shorts and yanked them down for her.

For him.

"Essie," Woods muttered in her ear, "you have a fantastic ass."

The thrill of praise made her smile, but it quickly dissolved when he slid his entire length into her in one quick, savage motion, hooking his fingers in her mouth and bending her over.

"Take it, take it, *take it,*" he snarled, his thrusts bitter, short, and merciless—like she'd been agitating him for weeks and he was finally taking out a wellspring of anger on her pussy.

The shocking ferocity made her cry out, the level of passion and touch—yes, just touch. Someone was touching her and it was affecting her so much, made her clench around his cock, her orgasm flickering and then catching fire, building to completion.

Her hands moved up and down on Levi's and Owen's cocks. Woods' shoved his dick in and out of her. The elevator moved up.

Floor 9.

She really wanted to cum. Woods was so warm, so firm—he withdrew once, groaning "Fuck, who would cheat on you?" before sliding back into her, his words punctuated as he gave her long, penetrating thrusts, the entire length of his cock exploring her. "So. Fucking. Hot."

Her thoughts were starting to become fragmented and sporadic as she dissolved into a state of constant stimulated reaction. Had she been moaning this entire time?

I'm being fucked senseless.

Floor 11.

Woods grabbed a tangle of her hair. "This what you wanted, you pathetic slut? Can you imagine if your friends knew what you were doing? The things they would say about you. The names they would call you.

Now she really, really wanted to cum.

"They'd call you a whore," Woods said in her ear.

Levi leaned in. "A cock-hungry bitch," he said.

"A worthless cunt," Owen added.

Floor 15.

"Oh my God, I'm going to cum, please don't stop—" Essie whined, bucking against Woods. The other men began pawing at her, Levi's hand rubbing her pussy as Woods bent her forward entirely, the new angle hitting a spot inside her that she'd never fully felt before. This was it. She was going to cum so fucking hard she passed out. *Fuck it, Essie, go into a coma, this is it--this is bliss, this is heaven, I could die right now—*

Floor 21.

She was so far from Ryan and the shore he was on.

She could still see it, faintly. The outline of him on his computer, ignoring her. The current had her completely. She was drowning, and loving every second of it.

"Tell me you want it," Woods said. She didn't think he was paying attention to what he was saying—he had been muttering and groaning with each thrust.

She twisted around and grinned at him. The words she meant to say tangled in her mouth as the orgasm started to work its way through her entire body.

"I want to drown in your cum," she told him. His mouth dropped open, his eyes rolling back slightly in ecstasy.

Floor 22.

The elevator dinged. The doors slid open.

Woods grinned and withdrew from her. Abruptly, the orgasm was cut off, the warm light in her blotted out. Essie's legs bucked, and she fell to the floor.

"No, no, no. Please keep going," she begged.

Owen and Levi picked her up and began carrying her down the hall. She was slung over Levi's shoulder, with Owen carrying her legs. She faced Woods as he walked behind them.

"You're not in control," Woods reminded her. "But if you keep saying things like that, you'll get whatever you want."

A hotel door opened and she was taken inside. The door closed behind her, and her only thought was that she was so glad she had called the number on that black card.

CHAPTER 7

She was expecting more talk; an elaborate charade where she was made to put on an outfit and parade about for them. A way of easing her into things.

They weren't interested in any of that.

Levi and Owen carried her to the bed and tossed her onto it. She sat up, just to be slammed back down by Woods, his chokehold firm and merciless. Essie wanted to ask him to take off the mask, but was interrupted by Levi kneeling between her legs, the cool plastic of the eyes of his mask grazing her naked thighs. Woods held her by the neck, forcing her to watch as Levi lifted his mask to expose his mouth, keeping it over the top of his head so she couldn't see his eyes.

His tongue was rough, wet, and so much longer than she expected. It seemed to grasp parts of her, running along crevices as she moaned and lifted her hips. He was close, so close to licking where she needed to be licked, he just had to—

Her head was shoved to the left, Owen's cock going into her mouth without hesitation as he kneeled on the bed next to her face. Gazing into his eyes, she swirled her tongue along the head of it, her hand sliding along the shaft and beginning to pump it. She tried to focus on those movements and only those movements, but then Levi clamped his entire warm, wet mouth around her pussy and *growled*, sending a thrill of vibrations into her so pleasurably that she gasped, sucking Owen's cock deeper into her throat. It made her gag, but that made *him* groan, his gloved hand caressing her face.

"Men have fantasies, too," Woods had told her. But that didn't prepare her for this. She expected them to take turns with her, or do separate, selfish things to her body. She hadn't expected this chemistry between them as they worked together, all to bring her concurrent waves of pleasure. It felt rehearsed, but intimate. Like they knew what they were doing but still enjoyed doing it.

Woods held her jaw firmly and began bobbing her head on Owen's cock. "Tighter. Make your lips tighter," he ordered. All of this while those black latex hands dove down the front of her body, his fingers spreading her pussy lips apart, holding her open so Levi's mouth could explore her more. The sensations all seemed to pulse in rhythm, a warm light flashing and growing brighter inside of her.

Owen's cock pumping between her lips, one of his arms bracing himself on the bed as he loomed over her.

Wood's hand around her neck, his words whispered to her. The mask flat against her earlobe, calling her a good girl, a goddess. "God Essie, you turn me on so much."

His middle and forefinger on his other hand slowly orbiting her clit, brushing it then leaving it alone just for Levi to lick it for a moment, the two of them alternating so perfectly it felt vindictive. Like they were playing a game with her body.

Levi's finger sliding in and out of her pussy.

The grunts, the breathing, the moans coming from each of them, the sounds she was making, all of it rising to a cacophony. It was too much—too much stimuli, too much going on, her entire perception narrowing to a pinpoint of pleasure, pressure imploding upon itself.

She threw her head back, Owen's cock dragging against her cheek. "I'm going to fucking *cum!*" she yelled at them angrily, like it was their fault (it was). As if it made her a little angry how good this felt (it did).

"Go ahead. Cum," Woods told her. "You can have the first one." He kept the same tempo, the same pressure on her clit. "The rest of them you will have to beg for."

She had to turn and scream into the pillow, her hands curling into fists that tore at the bedsheets, her legs tightening around the sides of Levi's head, grinding herself against his mouth as the orgasm ravaged her.

The pacing began to slow after that—Owen pulling away from her, Levi pulling his back over his mouth.

The pleasurable heat from all their bodies so close to her faded, and she looked around, desperate to know what was going to happen next. She watched as Levi took off his shirt and stood at the edge of the bed in nothing but a pair of black briefs, the mask still concealing his face. He took the gloves off, pulling them at the wrist with fluid ease that made her wonder if he worked in the medical field.

Owen left his gloves on as he stripped, the mask coming askew, forcing him to turn away slightly to readjust it.

Woods, however, stayed on the bed with her. He slid the bend of his elbow around her neck, squeezing her throat with his bicep. He forced her to sit up, and when she did, he maneuvered behind her, using his heels to hook into her thighs and pry her legs apart, her back against his chest as he turned her back and forth, seeming to relish the full control of her.

Black.

The safe word tempted her, but she didn't want to give Woods the satisfaction of tapping out so easily. This was a rush—a visceral, adrenalized blur of bodies and emotions, but the thirst to prove herself was still stronger than any sort of fear.

"Pick one," he said. "Pick who fucks you first."

That was easy; she wanted it to be Woods. The other two were fine. Wonderful. Particularly Levi if he kept doing that thing with his mouth. But she was here for Woods. If any of the other men had been the ones to greet her at the cafe, she wouldn't be here.

She enjoyed these greedy, lustful thoughts. Mechanisms of her brain that hadn't felt alive in years as the sex died its slow, painful death with Ryan.

Now she was being told to *pick*. The power made her nervous.

Essie wanted to lean back against Woods, knocking the mask off so she could speak clearly into his ear. *I want you to kick them out and make them listen to what you do to me. Make me scream so loudly they get hard just picturing what is happening.*

But, as she looked at Levi—his powerful chest, his bulging shoulders—she wondered if Woods ever got jealous. That would be delicious, getting him to drag her away from the other men in a frenzy of jealous lust. To claim her.

"I want Levi," she said.

Woods chuckled. "We'll never hear the end of it, will we, Owen?" His voice became deep, mocking Levi. "She chose me, bro. Did you see that?'"

Owen laughed. Was it her imagination or did Levi grow oddly still, like he wasn't in on the joke?

Woods released her and shoved her face down on the mattress. A swift slap made her ass sting.

Was there a little jealousy in that slap? A little frustration?

She didn't have time to overthink, because Levi was already pulling at her legs, dragging her to the edge of the bed, hands digging into her hips as he moved her easily.

Woods laid on his side, propping himself up with one hand, like he was lazily watching a football game on TV. The mask was askew at a jaunty angle, seeming to highlight how absurd this whole thing was.

That wouldn't do. She didn't want him lackadaisical

and aloof. She wanted him clenching his fists in anger.

She wanted him to remember her.

The weekend would end and they would all retreat back to their lives. Essie would go back to her collapsing relationship, Woods to the next client/volunteer/ kidnapping victim. Someone younger than her. Prettier. With better hair and a nicer smile. And she would be left rotting next to Ryan, or rebuilding her life piece by piece—all with the horrid sense that she had been wasted, wasted on men like Ryan, who said the right things and were dreadfully, painfully considerate and decent but still cheated.

Or wasted on someone like Woods, giving them some satisfaction for a small glimpse of time but not meeting whatever insane standard they had in a woman to be worthy of a relationship.

Her thoughts kept stacking; each delirium attaching itself to that horrific pit of rejection and shame that had been building for months. The one that grew larger each time she looked in the mirror and noticed a new line in the corner of her mouth, when whatever pants she chose that day fit too tightly or too loosely, when she passed a woman who dared to look happy *and* attractive. This pit of aching analysis—shredding her own skin with her eyes to grab the root of every flaw and hurl it—*splat*—against the mirrored glass and scream, "THIS! This is why he won't fuck me. This is why he found someone else."

She had taken a complete step towards mental collapse when she felt a hand on her shoulder. She looked over to see Woods, the mask perched on top of his head, revealing his warm, caring face crinkled into concern.

"Are you alright?"

"Yeah, I don't know, I'm fine."

He glanced at Levi. "Let's give her a break."

"Come on, we were just getting started," Levi protested.

"We have all night and tomorrow. Go get some water." He gave Essie another spank, but this one was light, affectionate. "Not everyone is a fucking degenerate, Levi. Some of us have emotions."

Levi groaned and slumped away, the door to the suite opening. Owen followed, closing the door behind him.

Woods hopped off the bed. "We'll leave you alone. If you want to leave, just let us know." He tilted his chin towards the phone next to the bed. "Order whatever you want."

He started to leave too, but she spoke.

"Can you stay?"

Woods grinned. "Only if I can brag to Levi and Owen that you like me more than them."

"Sure. Whatever makes you happy."

He fell back into bed, groaning with exhaustion. "I don't know the last time I just... laid down."

She settled next to him, pulling the covers over herself, their shoulders touching.

His face was half-buried into the pillow. "Your shampoo smells good," he said. "I can smell it on the pillow."

"Thank you. I spent an entire day getting ready."

"Yeah? We did that, too. I thought Owen was going to drown me with his cologne."

Her curiosity piqued. "You guys all get ready together? Like girls at a sleepover?"

"Kind of. It's easier than trying to pick everyone up the

night of." He reached over and brushed a sweaty strand of hair away from her eyes. "Organizing an orgy is more difficult than you think. Everyone is so busy these days."

"Do you all get ready in the same mirror and spray each other with cologne?" she teased. The bed felt like it was shrinking; the more they talked the more they naturally turned to each other—smiles widening, eyes darting around to search each other for detail.

"Yes, Essie, we all slap baby powder on each other's chests. I tell Owen he's a very good boy and Levi tells me how handsome I am." Woods' face crinkled in amusement before he burst into a delighted laugh. "When Owen first started doing this, he was so scared about us seeing his dick."

"*Really?*"

"Oh yeah, this is good gossip. Don't tell him I said this, he'll be mad. He thought we were like... pornstars."

"What does that mean?"

"Giant cocks."

"Oh." She started to compliment his, then realized she hadn't actually seen it.

"He thought we had these massive, mutant pieces and he wouldn't measure up. He tried to back out, saying the women wouldn't want him."

"His cock is, uh... very nice."

Woods nestled closer to her, one arm snaking over, just under her breasts, pulling her closer to him. Their noses touched briefly as he spoke softly. "You should tell him that."

The nervousness was dissipating. The world had stopped spinning. Her emotional hurricane still lingered, but maybe she was in the eye of the storm right now. She let her voice drop, becoming soft, and whispered. "Yeah? Won't I make you jealous?"

His hand was on her hip now. "Hmm, depends on how you say it."

She leaned into him, her leg hooking over his, drawing his knee between her thighs as she sidled up to him, falling into the nook under his chin, against his chest. Her lips trailed towards his ear, kissing gently, feeling the rasp of his stubble. "You have a really, really nice cock," she said softly.

He squeezed her ass, his knee firm against her pussy. "That might make me jealous," he murmured. And then they were kissing, angrily, like they'd just broken up but realized the mistake and wanted to be back together, a chaotic clatter of lips and tongue and teeth. Her fingernails dug into his collarbone as his hands moved over her body, squeezing and touching, never staying in one spot for long, as if he couldn't decide which part of her he wanted to touch the most.

His hands moved to her breasts, and for a moment he paused, moving his fingers over one of her nipples, his entire hand laying flat with the nipple poking between his middle and ring finger. He squeezed them together, trapping it, and pulled on it slightly, the rest of his hand grabbing her breast.

"Are you alright now?" he asked. His tone was teasing, but there was concern on his face.

"Mmhm," she groaned, turning to lay flat on her back, hoping he would do the same thing to her other breast. As if he read her mind, his hand moved to it, giving it the same teasing treatment.

"You want to keep going?"

"Yes."

He slapped her. It was firm enough but didn't sting at all. It knocked her chin towards him, so she could glare in his eyes. "What are your safe words?"

"Black."

He gathered her wrists and locked them together, pinning them above her head. He got on top of her, leaning his entire weight down. "And what does that mean?"

"It means I'm enjoying it but would like to move on."

"Open your mouth."

She let her jaw drop.

"What is the second?"

"Black card."

He spit into her mouth, some of the saliva landing on her chin. He clamped a palm over her lips, his forehead pressing directly against her forehead. Essie groaned, rubbing her thighs together underneath him. She'd always wondered what this was like. Ryan might utter a "right there, baby" during sex but he'd never had the patience—the sense of the moment—to do anything like this.

"What does black card mean, Essie?" He removed his hands from her mouth and stared intently at her.

"It means... It means I am uncomfortable and want you to do something else immediately."

More slaps, back and forth across her face. He was being such a dick. Genuine anger flared in her, only to be silenced when he choked her—the air clicking in her throat, her feet kicking as she struggled for air.

He held her for a long pause. His eyes moved rapidly in their sockets, examining every movement of her face. She could feel how hard he was, pressing against her leg.

"If you're being choked, like this..." he said, tightening even more, "Or there's something in your mouth, how do you communicate you need help?

Essie stopped struggling and blinked rapidly, five times.

"Good girl." He released his grip.

She coughed when he let go, drawing in rough gulps of air.

Woods sat up and slid off the bed. He wandered to the foot of it, his fingers brushing her toes. Leaning on an elbow, she watched him.

"And the last one?"

"Black card, black card."

"And that means?"

"Full stop. Everything ends. You'll take me home."

He was putting the mask back on. "Are you ready?"

No. Not really. She should be home, wrapped in a blanket, making an attempt at reading a book but actually just scrolling on her phone.

But Woods looked so damn good in that mask.

"I'm ready."

He knocked twice on the bedroom door. Owen and Levi walked through it.

"Do either of you have a pen?" Woods asked.

Owen reached into his pocket and pulled out a black permanent marker.

Woods took it. He flipped it in his hand. "Good

enough." He looked at Essie. The mask, the change in demeanor... It was hard to believe that moments ago he had been gentle. Tender. Almost loving. "Grab her."

Levi and Owen pounced on her. She drew her legs back in mock-terror, glaring at them. Owen grabbed her wrist; she twisted out of it, only to have Levi seize her ankles and drag her off the bed.

Her resistance seemed to baffle them. Levi glanced at Woods, who shrugged.

"She knows the safe words. If she wants to be disobedient, we can fix that."

She was forced to her knees. Levi held her right arm, one hand clamped tightly around her shoulder, the other grasping her wrist. Owen did the same on her left.

Woods crouched in front of her and uncapped the marker. She twisted away, but the men didn't budge.

In jagged, black letters, Woods wrote "S-L-U-T" across her naked chest, starting the S high near her collarbone and dragging the top of the T over her nipple and down her breast.

She looked down and gaped at it. The chemical smell of the marker wafted into her nostrils. "Is that permanent? Please tell me that it wasn't permanent."

"It'll wash off. Eventually." He stood and capped the pen before tossing it onto the little desk. "After your husband sees it."

That sent a jolt of anger through her she didn't quite understand. Who the fuck did this man think he was? A two-bit, Christian Grey rip-off in a Halloween mask—

"We made her mad," Woods said, amused.

"Good," Levi replied. Together he and Owen pulled

her up by the arms, until she was trapped between the three men, each of them forming the points of a rough triangle. "She looks hot when she's angry."

She glanced wildly to each one, feeling the pinpricks of fear, the wild thud in her chest of excitement. There was an intensity here she didn't know was possible. It was still tempting to cry out, "Black card, black card," but now she wanted to see how far they would take this.

How far they would take her.

She was shoved in the back by Owen, so that she pressed against Levi's chest. Someone—she wasn't sure who—positioned themselves directly behind her, her ass pressing against an erection, their breath on her back and neck.

She was squeezed between them, looking up into Levi's merciless eyes.

Woods, somewhere to the left—that meant it was Owen directly behind her, groping her breasts, his erection stiff against her—said, "I'm getting bored. Will someone stick their cock in this little cunt already?"

I don't understand. How is he so sweet and gentle one minute, then a raging dickhead the next?

Was it all manipulation? Was he sweet talking her into doing whatever he wanted? Was there any truth to how he was in the bed?

There was no time—thank God—to overanalyze her favorite masked man because the other two seemed intent on tearing her apart. She found herself suspended between them, her arms around Levi's neck, her legs hooked around his hips as she sank down with a yelp onto his cock.

The blank face of the mask made his thrusts impersonal. She was being used; whatever this man was in real life, this was what he looked forward to. She was his toy right now, a thing to be to fucked to relieve stress. She felt the rigid hardness of his arms, the coiled strength, and wondered if she could get him to beg for her.

Getting someone like that to submit would be addicting.

Levi kept fucking her, but by natural motion and the weight of them together he gradually sank lower and lower to the floor, eventually lying flat on his back. Owen's hands on her shoulders helped them keep balance until she was sitting on top of Levi, rocking with the motion of his hips as he kept powering into her from below. He kept hold of her sides, his palms firm against her ribs as he moved her up and down on his dick. He raised her until it nearly slipped out, the head of it stretching her entrance, before letting her slide back down. He growled each time, his words getting lost and nonsensical in a jumble of pleasure. "Right, just like that, right there—"

Woods and Owen approached her from either side, stroking their cocks.

"I thought you could ride dick better than that, Essie." Woods said.

Keeping her eyes locked on him, she began rolling her hips on top of Levi, meeting his thrusts. Still not breaking eye contact, she leaned forward and took Owen in her mouth. She let out a loud moan, just for Woods' benefit, before making a luxurious show of slowly nodding her head, the ridges and veins on Owen bumping against her lips.

Woods watched this for a while, lazily stroking himself. Once, he seemed to yawn, his chest swelling and a great sigh emanating from behind the mask.

She let go of Owen with a loud *pop,* even as Levi began pumping faster from below, each jolt sending that aching, stuffed feeling deeper and deeper into her stomach, making it hard to talk.

"Am I boring you?" she asked him.

He replied by slapping her with his cock. "Open."

Levi kept fucking her, this time bouncing her so that Wood's dick brushed her forehead.

"Stop," Woods told him.

Levi froze. He and Essie both came to a panting standstill. He was still buried inside of her, and started to do tiny, micro thrusts that made her dig her nails into his forearms.

"Owen," Woods said. "Get me the whip."

Owen disappeared for a moment, then came back, handing him a black whip.

"Now," Woods said, uncoiling it. "Essie, put your arms behind your back." She did so. "Levi, hold her hands."

Levi reached his broad arms around her and clamped his hands over hers. "Open your mouth, Essie."

She did so.

He placed his cock gently in her mouth. She clamped her lips around it, eager to hear him gasp.

The whip cracked, striking her ass with stinging viciousness. She hissed, baring her teeth around his cock.

"Oh, you want to use your teeth? Okay." He laid the whip over his shoulder and took control of her head. "Bite the tip. Bite it."

She bit down, gingerly, using her front teeth, not wanting to hurt him.

The whip struck her again.

"Come on! Bite it, you little slut! Harder!"

She bit down all the way and he roared in a mixture of pain and satisfaction. "Finally! Jesus fucking Christ—" The whip came down again and again. "When I tell you–" *Crack.* "—to do something—" *Crack.* "—you'd better do it."

He gave the whip to Owen. "She disobeys again, give it to her. Hard." He gazed at Essie. "But she's going to be very good from now on, right?"

Her eyes, full of tears, stayed on him. "Yes, sir."

"Open your mouth. Do *not* close it until I say."

Her mouth hung open, anxious and waiting as he began to fuck her throat.

Levi was below her still. She could sense his frustration; he'd been fucking her in short, spasmic bursts whenever Woods seemed distracted.

"Do you like Levi's cock in you, Essie?"

"Yes, sir. I love it." She said, muffled, trying to form the words around his cock. It drew laughter from the men.

"He's a good boy, isn't he?"

The sense of control, the confident dominance emanating from Woods... It seemed like an average work day to him. Her wildest, most fucked up fantasies were routine to him. He took his cock out of her mouth and waited for her to speak.

Her response was automatic, subdued. "Yes, he's very good."

He forced her mouth back onto his cock but held her still. "Levi, I want you to fuck her slowly. Shove your dick in her so deep that it makes her toes curl. I'm going to do the same to her throat." His fingers trailed absently through her hair. "You need to match my speed, Levi. If you don't... Well, I guess I'll just have to take it out on Essie."

Levi lifted his hips, arching his back, balancing with his legs, his dick stretching her out, the friction making her dizzy with pleasure, with that sense of being *filled,* even as Woods held her in a viselike grip, holding her chin, keeping her mouth wide as he shoved himself all the way in. Her forehead touched his stomach as he leaned over her, a low groan of pleasure escaping him. She squeezed her eyes shut, willing herself not to gag.

Levi's hips contracted, pulling out of her halfway. Woods did the same, except he pulled out of her mouth, a long strand of saliva forming a hanging line between the tip of his cock and her lips.

He took the whip back from Owen. "Again," Woods said, and she braced herself as they both entered her again, harder this time.

CRACK!

The whip snapped across her back, ripping a scream out of Essie. She looked up at Woods—her eyes full of tears, saliva coating his cock as she kept her lips against it while she pleaded with him. "What? What? Please just tell me what to do." The thrill of the whip coming down at any moment was causing her nerves to jangle and fray, adrenaline leaping in her chest and she tried to anticipate it.

Woods seemed pleased with himself. "You're doing amazing. Levi went a little too fast."

85

They did it over again, Woods taunting Levi, asking if his dick was getting smaller and if that was as far as he could get inside of her.

"Please," Essie said, "I am so close, can he just—"

"You want him to fuck you faster? Is that it?"

"Yes, God yes, please—"

"You'll have to beg Levi, not me. I'm sure if you ask him very, very nicely, and tell him how much you love his cock, then he'll take care of you."

Essie laid on Levi, flattening herself against his chest. Her hair fell over him as she nudged the mask away from his ear and whispered, "Please, Levi. You feel so good..." She paused, fumbling for the words to say. Trying to sound sexy felt as impossible as trying to be funny. Every word ridiculous, like a movie scene. Every syllable seemed as though someone was going to yell "Cut," so Essie and the men could roll their eyes at each other.

She decided to just ask for what she wanted. "Can you fuck me harder?"

The mask tilted to face her. His hands caressed her face. His palms cupped her chin, thumbs trailing her lips as he made her lean back and settle on his cock again.

"Please..." Essie was getting impatient. She began grinding her hips on him, his thighs making a clapping sound against her ass each time she slammed herself down, picking up the pace, another orgasm flickering and threatening to catch light—

His caress tightened into an angry grip around her throat. "Stop talking. I'm going to cum if I hear another word outta you."

She grinned and started to say something else, but

Owen covered her mouth with his palm. "Fuck her how she wants. It's my turn next," he said. Her head was tilted backwards, so that she was staring up into Owen's mask as Levi's cock assaulted her from below.

Maybe they were just acting. Playing their roles. Maybe they got off on the power or simply enjoyed wearing masks and group-fucking sad, desperate women.

But having them talk this way about her... Treat her this way... This worship, this brutal, direct desire... After months—*years*—of watching Ryan drift away, of examining herself in the mirror and wondering what had happened to the days when his hands wouldn't leave her. Was she used up? Had she wasted away as the birthdays rolled on, as new frown lines formed like tally marks against her soul? Everyone rallied against the programming, of course. You're beautiful at twenty-nine, at thirty-five, at forty. You are woman, eternal, everyone waving the social media pom-poms and cheering each other on, but that doesn't change the fact that suddenly your husband wants someone else, that you spent so much of your life etching yourself into someone fuckable for him and he throws it all away.

And then three men in masks, with their muscles rippling, their breathing heavy and hot as they touch you, fuck you, tell you they can't wait to do obscene things to you...

It was incredible. It was the feeling of getting a text after a first date, asking for a second. That exhilaration, that great relief. She felt it on her wedding day, when he blinked and said, "You look like an angel." And guess what? He fucking ruined it, so let these men use her. Let them treat her like a goddess *and* as a toy. She would fuck them however they wanted and each time they brought her to orgasm it would be another door slamming shut and locking between her and Ryan.

Somewhere, a phone rang.

Hers. The ringer cut through the mood like a false note. Reality, ringing in, telling her to come home. Owen, Levi, and Essie each froze, glancing around for the intruding noise.

Woods crossed the room and unzipped her backpack. He held the phone out, letting it chime loudly. He looked back at them. "Why'd you stop? Keep going." He brought it over, peeling the mask away from his face. He was grinning. "It's just her husband."

Owen held her. Levi fucked her. And Woods held the ringing screen to her face as she bobbed up and down on Levi's cock, looking at her husband's picture, his face tilted sheepishly at the camera the way he always did when she took his photos.

Ryan wasn't hanging up. The phone sent it to voicemail. The screen went dark, as if gathering its thoughts. After a moment, it lit again. The jaunty green phone icon greeting her. *Answer me, answer me, tell me what you've been doing.*

"Answer it," Woods ordered.

She twisted away from Owen's dick and shook her head.

"Should I answer it?" Woods asked. "I'll describe to him exactly what your pussy feels like. How it clenched when you were close to cumming. 'Ryan, have you ever fucked your wife in an elevator? Let me tell you—'" A cruel grin stretched across Woods' face. "Answer it, or I will."

She snatched the phone out of his hand, her mouth twisted in a frown of disgust. She did her best to catch her breath, even as all the motion with Levi inside of her threatened another orgasm.

She swiped on the green icon and held the phone to her ear.

"Hey," Ryan said—too casually, too genuinely. "I just wanted to check in on you."

Such sincerity. He was lying; he knew something was off and this was his way of keeping tabs on her.

"That's sweet of you," Essie replied. Levi did something with his hips and she had to bite down on her lip to keep from moaning.

"Are you sure? I know things have been... tense between us. Work's been getting to me and—" He prattled on, but she lost track as Owen shoved his dick into her mouth and pulled it out, then turned her head to face Woods, who did the same. She glared up at him, mustering every bit of loathing she could even as she tightened her lips around him and lathered him with her tongue.

"Good girl, listen to your husband," Woods muttered. His eyes were bright, excited. "She gives better head when he's on the phone, don't you think? Try her mouth again, Owen."

She had time to gasp before Owen explored her mouth again, this time jamming himself against the inside of her cheek.

"You okay?" Ryan asked.

Essie seized Owen's cock and shoved it away. "Yeah," she panted into the phone. Levi began fucking her, hard.

These men were trying to make her scream. They didn't care if she got caught; it seemed to excite them. "Yeah, I'm fine. We're outside, we went for drinks and then for a walk."

"Sounds fun. What are you drinking?"

Why do you give a fuck, Ryan? Did your slut not pick up the phone when you called? Are you worried that I'm out here cheating on you? Don't worry, I'm not cheating. I promise.

I'm getting fucking railed. Not just by one, but by three men. I haven't even seen all of their faces and I already like them better than I like you. And you know what? I love it. I love how they use me. How they want me. I almost wish you were here, to see me on my knees, my hair a mess, my mascara running. You should see how red my ass is from them spanking me. The marks on my neck from being choked. I'm their whore, and I love it. I hope you can hear it in my voice.

"Oh, just cocktails."

Woods laughed. Ryan heard it, too.

"Who's that, a new friend?"

"Just a guy in the background, dear. You have nothing to worry about." As she said it, she leaned forward, giving Woods that hungry glare, and took his balls into her mouth. Her free hand grabbed Levi's arm and guided his hand to her tits, making him squeeze her. She wanted all of their hands on her, right now, as her husband blabbered mindlessly on the phone.

"Okay! Well, I just wanted to call and see how you were doing—"

His words faded from meaning, because as he started talking, Woods leaned down and kissed her. When the kiss broke, Ryan was still talking in her ear. Woods nuzzled against her and spoke in the other.

"If he calls again, he's going to hear how you sound with all three of us inside of you at once."

She stared directly into Woods' eyes, tracing his pupils with her gaze, trying to find a hint of a joke. That was a taunt, one of Wood's "escalate the moment" teasings, but he wouldn't actually do that, right?

He matched her stare, beat for beat.

He was telling the truth.

"Hey, Ryan?" she said. "I have to go but um…"

Woods' teeth bit down on her shoulder.

She held back a growl of pleasure. "Call me back later, please."

CHAPTER 8

Essie had always wanted to live inside of a music video.

Adult life had filled rapidly with a sort of monotony she found appalling, and vaguely terrifying. More and more her days were eaten away by meaningless tasks. Oil changes. Doctor's appointments. Waiting in line for coffee. Waiting in line to get lunch. The DMV. Waiting for her husband to get home; waiting for him to go to sleep so she could let the mask of "everything is fine, dear, really" fall.

Waiting and wasting.

She wanted jump cuts. Scene fades, every boring aspect of being alive snipped neatly away. A highlight reel of her life, never existing in those dreaded moments of in-between.

For a moment—with Woods, Owen, and Levi—she got that.

After she hung up the phone, the structure of everything dissolved. Hands carried her back to the bed. She remembered the springs of the mattress creaking, the headboard slapping against the wall as all four of them laid upon it, the men forming a loose pile on top of her.

She couldn't keep up with it all.

It became both image and sensation. The things that were happening to her fading rapidly into memory almost before they even happened.

Owen and Levi, taking turns with their mouths on her pussy. Woods covering her eyes and demanding she pick which tongue she liked best (Levi's).

Kissing Woods even as Levi buried his face in her ass.

Each of them taking turns in missionary, one after another. Levi muttering something sweet about her hair in her ear, Owen complimenting her lips, Woods telling her they never usually went this long. Normally everyone tired out, there was just something about *her*. "Fuck, Essie, why'd you have to be so hot? I might not let you go. I might keep you on a leash forever."

Exhausted, her entire body sore, and none of the men seeming close to slowing down, she managed to utter, "Black Card."

They each froze in what they were doing and looked up. It struck her as comical, how obedient they were. Woods was wearing his mask again, so three Jason Voorhees characters looked at her, bewildered.

Almost innocent.

She pulled away from Woods, and detangled herself from Owen and Levi, the jumble of human bodies suddenly claustrophobic and oppressive.

"I'm sorry," she said, gulping from the water bottle next to the bed. "I am so tired. I can't do anymore."

Woods nodded, and led her gently into the next room, the large suite opening into the living room area. Over the plush, soft carpets, he showed her the bathroom, with its gleaming whirlpool tub and sterile, minimalist-grey tile. "Take a bath. Rest. We'll make the bed for you." He turned the water on, leaning over the edge of the tub. She could see deep scratches in his back.

My nails did that.

There was a certain level of triumph in the thought.

"Do you like the water hot? I try to melt the skin off my bones when I shower, but everyone's different—"

"Scalding, please," she said, smiling at him. He'd done it again; switching from a sex fiend to someone caring, jovial. Running her bath water.

He held her hand and helped her into the water. Waited until she was settled in, the foaming white bubbles rising to her chin. Her body sank into the near-unbearable heat, and every muscle went *ahhh* as it relaxed. She closed her eyes and felt sleep tugging at her.

"Do you need anything else, Essie?"

"Mmm, no. I'm sorry I can't keep going. I want to, I'm just…"

"You're okay." He knelt next to the tub, resting his chin on his folded arms as he watched her. "I think the guys were trying to impress you, so they did their best to make it last."

She opened one eye. "Were you trying to impress me, too?"

"Absolutely. Did it work?"

"Eh, you're alright."

He laughed, dipped his fingers in the water, then flicked them at her. "Shut up. Let me know if you need anything."

"Actually, my phone. My friend will worry."

He nodded, disappeared quickly through the door, then came back and handed her cellphone over, flicked more water at her, and left. There were text messages from Carly, threatening police and the United Nations if she didn't call her soon.

Quickly, before she fell asleep, she called Carly.

Carly's voice, aloud, alarmed. "Please tell me you're alive and about to be in a post-sex coma." Her friend sounded scared, but was hiding it with a joke.

"I'm okay. Tired, though. Very, very tired."

"They're being good to you?"

"So good. Listen, I have to go, I'm... busy."

"I get it. I'll call off the bomb threat I made to the hotel."

Essie let Carly go and slid further into the water. It was too cozy in this tub. She wanted to wake up, go out there and see what else the men had planned for her. But the water, the soap, the heat, all held her tightly. A few hours ago, falling asleep among masked strangers would've been cause for a panic attack.

But she could hear Woods talking to the men in the next room. The gentle boom of his voice, the occasional laugh, the clatter of something being moved.

There was no lingering resentment lurking, like at her house. No uncertainty in where she stood. The radioactive tension was gone.

It made it so easy to sleep.

There's a dream-like, half-reality you swim in when your alarm clock goes off and you hit snooze. Vaguely aware of the world, but you're building your perception of it on the scaffolds of sleep, so everything has a hazy, half-remembered, discolored sensation to it.

Essie was in this as she either dreamed or remembered Woods coming back a while later, picking her up out of lukewarm, nearly cold water. Drying her with a warm, soft white towel before wrapping her in a robe and carrying her back to the bed. She was laid in fresh clean sheets. She remembered being puzzled by that. Did they change them? But her head hit the pillow, and she had time to think, *hmm, this pillowcase smells like Woods*, before she was out, out *hard*, the only apt description being *coma* for how hard she slept.

But she awoke to an argument.

The little digital alarm clock next to the king-sized bed glared 2:09 AM as the heated, muffled voices reached her from behind the closed door. She could hear them talking, pacing back and forth in the living room of the suite. A TV was playing—she heard the sound of swords clanging.

She sat up, the covers spilling off her, and crawled to

the edge of the bed.

"Sit down and watch the movie," Woods was saying.

"I didn't come here to watch movies," Levi replied.

Essie went to the door and pressed her ear against it.

"We saw what she selected on the form. She's up for anything," Owen said.

"She's sleeping," Woods said. He sounded closest to the door. The image forming in her head was of him, not wearing a mask, his back to her door as he stood between her and the other men, each wearing their masks, leering at him.

"She checked *everything*, man. Let me wake her up with my dick in her mouth," Levi's voice was sharp, demanding.

Woods, on the other hand, sounded like a patient camp counselor. "I know. But you saw her; she was exhausted after two hours. She's been sleeping like a rock, I put her in the bed and she didn't even know where she was."

"She called us," Owen said. "She wants this."

"Stop," Woods replied. "Yeah, she checked 'anything and everything.' But you know how this goes. She was upset at her life and wanted to do something risky."

"We're just trying to have fun—"

"Levi, you're like seven feet tall and look like you can throw a fridge. I get that you guys don't really talk to the girls we bring here but have *some* sense, please."

Owen, closer to the door now. "We're not going to hurt her—"

"*She* doesn't know that. And if you two idiots barge in there and jump on her, you're gonna scare the fuck out of her."

"I think you like her." Levi, even closer to the door.

She had a brief flash of a daydream; Levi and Owen shoving Woods aside, bursting through the door and catching her listening. Levi—menacing—saying, "Looks who's out of bed," before the two of them seized her and relentlessly fucked her—

"Yeah, she's cool. I also know this is probably the craziest thing she's done in her entire life. So, we're going to take it easy. Let her rest."

Someone grumbled an unintelligible sentence.

Woods laughed. "I know, I want another piece of her too. And if she keeps looking at Levi like that, I'll get jealous."

The tone shifted; the men moved away from the door. The TV got louder, but she heard Woods say, "We have the toys for tomorrow, right?"

She awoke with hands around her throat and a voice in her ear.

Woods.

"It's time to get up," he whispered. "We aren't done with you."

Bright sunshine streamed into the room. The smell of toast and coffee in the room. Woods let go of her and strolled around the room as she rubbed her eyes and sat up. Food was on silver trays at the foot of the bed.

"Eat," he said. He pointed to the dresser by the window. "There's an outfit in there. Put it on. When you're ready, join us in the living room."

She sat there, struggling to wake up. The events of the previous night were still completing their download; she had an assortment of images and sensations to sort through later.

For now, though, the shock of seeing Woods, being reminded he was real, like a delicious nightmare you managed to have a second time, got her moving. She nibbled on some toast as she stretched and wandered the room, stopping to open the dresser. She found a simple pair of tennis shorts, with a black collar and chain leash resting on top of it.

She placed these on the bed and looked at them, arms crossed.

One hand, it was nice that they hadn't decided to put her in some elaborate, stringy lingerie that felt like doing a yarn puzzle, trying to figure out what bit of cloth covered which part of her body, just to wind up chafed and uncomfortable because she put it on wrong. Which she would do. Multiple times.

But the collar and leash were a bit much. Maybe it was the daylight; maybe her endorphins weren't hitting her and the excitement of the moment had faded, but this... This was insane. It would be better to go and leave now, think about things.

She grabbed her phone and felt a sense of relief. Here was reality: 12 missed texts from Carly, a missed call from Ryan, a litany of other notifications.

She answered Carly's latest text, *just let me know you're ok* with *I promise, I'm fine. Black card.*

She started to answer the others. Started to text Ryan.

The gravity of her life threatened to drag her back in. The person she was– *there* –trying to push out who she was— *here.*

Back there, she was low. An ignored wife. The quiet friend. Trying so goddamned hard to be loved.

Here, she was worshiped.

Here, she had men trying to get past each other to taste her.

Maybe it wasn't healthy. Maybe it was dangerous. A toxic fire waiting to be lit.

Essie wanted it anyway.

She ducked into the attached bathroom, hurriedly cleaning herself up and reapplying makeup. Last night, there'd been time. Hours to prepare. To try different eyeshadows and lipsticks. Now, it was like she was getting ready for a first date that was already at her door. She rapidly applied it, frowning at her results the entire time before dashing back into the bedroom. The robe came off, the shorts went on. She walked to the mirror to examine how she was going to look with the collar on.

And stopped dead.

Catching herself in the mirror was like getting caught in a bear trap. All momentum halted so you could focus on a particular body part and analyze that pain. Sometimes it was your legs, not toned enough. Sometimes it was your face—why was it *that* shape? Maybe your nose hung like an ugly Christmas ornament between your eyebrows. Maybe your eyebrows had that furry caterpillar look, or maybe they weren't perfectly even. They never fucking were. Chest was always too flat or too saggy, shoulders seemed mannish, every optical illusion in the world activated in that hotel mirror. As if it were a cruel funhouse reflection.

You're oozing out of those shorts, Essie. Look how your hips spill over the side. Just like cupcakes when they swell in the pan.

Look at those marks, those stretch marks on your stomach. Your skin literally shows scars because of how gross you are. What are you doing here? You know this is all an act; you're not this person. Woods isn't attracted to you. Levi isn't. Owen. They're going to laugh when it's over. They'll high-five and say, "Can't believe we got through that."

You're charity.

A pity fuck.

They're counting on you to go tell someone prettier how well you were treated.

The confidence she'd managed to build was getting shot down. It was an airplane over enemy territory, rocking with gunfire from the ground. The shorts cut into her flesh; the elastic waistband might've been barbed wire for how it sliced into her. Her thighs bulged out of the legs. Her knees had a doughy, loose quality to them that she couldn't quite place but hated all the same.

Her eyes roamed the landscape of her own body and wished it could be leveled. No canyons, no creases. Smoothed over and perfect. A parking lot.

Woods knocked on the door.

"Are you okay?" he asked.

"Yep. I'm fine." The words sounded passable to her. The little sob between "yep" and "fine" didn't help, but there was no way he heard it—

He slipped into the room and quietly closed the door. He was shirtless, maskless, wearing a small silver chain around his neck. He examined the expression on her face, and she watched him shift from confusion to concern.

"What's wrong? Did we do something?"

Essie snatched the robe and threw it over herself. She sat down heavily on the bed, her shoulders slumped. "I looked in the mirror."

He glanced at it. "Ah." He began checking his own reflection, moving his shoulders around, bobbing his head to check different angles. "I look at these things, and one minute, I'm gorgeous, right? Like a genuinely hot guy." He touched his hair. "Then, I look in a different mirror. Or my phone camera, that's the worst. Photos. I can't stand it. Like, let me live in delusion. Don't show me that I look like that."

"So, you understand that when I try to wear this... Now, in the broad daylight, looking at that mirror, I..."

He started nodding, approaching her on the bed. Her knees bumped against his as he laid both hands on the mattress and leaned over her. Her neck leaned back to keep his gaze, like she was sitting front row in a movie theater, and he was the screen.

"I get it. I also know that I had to keep Levi and Owen from coming in here in the middle of the night and fucking you until you couldn't move." He leaned down further, his face next to hers, his mouth near her ear. "So cut the bullshit and get out here so I can cover you in my cum."

She had a retort, but his final words made them dissolve. She could only glare at him in shock. She'd been expecting comfort, compliments. She wouldn't have believed them and she would have disregarded them immediately, of course, but still…

Would have been nice.

Instead, she reacted as if she had been slapped. He gave her a dismissive roll of the eyes and left the room, pausing at the door to say, "You have five minutes. Don't make us come in here."

She sat on the bed, biting her nails. The collar and leash next to her.

She stood up, ignoring the mirror.

There was a chance Woods was just saying whatever he could to get her out there.

But she chose to believe he meant it.

Essie snapped the black collar around her neck. The silver chain hung heavily between her breasts. She went to the door, stopped, thought about it, and pushed the door open.

The men were back in their masks. Levi was on the couch, his legs spread, revealing his bulge against his dark blue boxers. Owen was in the corner, leaning against the wall, shirtless, wearing black jeans.

Only Woods was fully clothed, wearing a white button up and slacks. The mask stood out against his formal attire. He was sitting in the armchair, angled towards her bedroom door.

She sank to her knees, placing the chain in her mouth, biting down on it gently with her teeth, holding it in place.

Levi began stroking himself, watching her.

Essie crawled to the men in the masks, already wet at the thought of what they might do to her.

CHAPTER 9

She expected them to be rough; like wolves falling on a sheep. She expected—even wanted—to be torn apart a little. She thought she'd be struggling to take someone's cock while another one of them forced her to give them head. She expected slaps and taunts—Woods to be the cruel, dominant man he'd been before.

Instead, Woods gestured for her to crawl to him. She did so, teasingly, letting the chain fall in his lap.

"Come here," he said quietly.

She rose, and he guided her to sit on his lap, her back against his chest, so that she could look out at the other men. Both of his hands found her breasts and squeezed, her nipples hardening between his fingers.

"They can't wait to have you," Woods told her. "*I* can't wait. We've barely slept, we've been too excited." He reached down and parted her thighs; the crotch of the shorts pulled aside too, revealing her to Owen and Levi. Woods spread her open. "We can't decide what we like most. Your pussy or your mouth."

She groaned, arching her back against him, pressing into his body. The lack of confidence was disappearing; something about Woods made her feel like an entirely new person. His praise wasn't insincere. It was firm and eager.

She began playing with herself, locking eyes with Owen, and then Levi, putting on a pleased smile as she massaged her clit. Woods was getting hard against her.

"I almost don't want to share you," he muttered in her ear. Softly, so only she could hear. "I want to lock you in that room with me—*just* me—and make you scream my name so loudly the others know there's no point in fucking you. You belong to *me.*"

Please do it. Take me, take me right now, don't let me leave, don't let me go home. Let me be your pet for the rest of my life.

"But I don't want to wait another second," he said. He pulled his cock out of his pants and pressed it against her pussy, letting her lips grip the head, letting every groove of her feel every inch of him as he slid into her with one slow thrust, her hips sinking down onto his thighs as she let out a soft gasp, relishing the familiar thrill from when he first had her in the elevator. Levi was big and Owen was nice, but Woods' cock managed to hit her in a different spot. She didn't know if it was the curve or the shape or just the way he moved his body, but it felt more urgent, more sincere.

Like he wanted her more.

She leaned forward to take more of him and he kissed between her shoulder blades, a warm wet kiss that brought a smile to her face. She started riding him, doing her best to raise herself before letting gravity take her back down on his dick, letting it go deeper each time.

"That's it, Essie," he said, his lips moving against her spine now. "Put on a show for them. Let them know who's your favorite."

She moaned and moved her body faster. Woods's hands held her thighs far apart, and he titled his hips so his cock could go in deeper, hitting her spot at a new angle, the sensation refreshed, a new jolt of sweetness that was rapidly erasing all coherent thought from her mind.

Essie leaned back and pressed her cheek against his, her head tipped so her hair spilled over the back of the chair. His arms rose and held her around her stomach, his cock pumping into her from below in short, frantic thrusts.

"Am I *your* favorite, Woods?" She said this softly. Shyly. "Tell me. Tell me I'm better than the other girls you bring here." She didn't care if he had to lie, didn't care if other women had done far more than her. She just wanted to hear that she impressed him. At least a little.

"You have 'slut' written on your chest. You're wearing a fucking leash." He dug his fingers into her thighs. "You're not just my favorite. I want to keep you forever."

They found each other for a kiss, but he broke it off abruptly, muttering, "Goddamn it," into her shoulder. She felt his breathing hitch and he thrust into her so hard the neatly trimmed hair around his groin brushed against her pussy, tickling it as he held it there. He pumped his hips one more time, and then came inside of her.

There was so much of it, it came dribbling back down his cock as he kept at it with a few apologetic pumps, even as he mumbled, "I'm sorry, I didn't mean to—"

It was dizzying, the shot of confidence it gave her, knowing he couldn't control himself when he felt her. The power, the affirmation. She'd been at the mercy of this man, essentially from the time they first met, and now he was apologizing to her about finishing too quickly.

All because of her.

Essie from the suburbs.

Essie with the husband who didn't want her.

She didn't have to revel in her victory, because Levi and Owen were pulling her off of Woods, the chain around her neck looped around Levi's fists.

"We took it easy on you last night," Levi remarked.

It was easier to be playful with Levi. He didn't stir the complex cauldron of emotions like Woods did.

She settled on her knees and blinked her eyes at him. "I was taking it easy on you, too."

Levi made her stand. Woods settled back in the chair and watched, his cum leaking out of her, making her feel marked and used. The chain around her neck, "SLUT" inked across her chest, cum dripping down her thighs... Each element of this scene driving home the fact that when she went back to Ryan, she'd be a very, very different woman.

Levi placed both of his massive hands on her hips and

lifted her off the ground. She was tossed onto the couch, landing on her back—trying to sit up, but already getting slammed back down by Levi, his bulging arms taking her wrists and pinning them against her chest. He was already fucking her, her eyes rolling with pleasure as his massive cock pushed through the mess Woods left inside of her. Levi pressed her into the couch cushions and sank into her, the couch starting to slide with the force of his body, making him grab the back of it to hold it still, leaving her nowhere to go, no choice but to take it. Sweat glistened on his bare chest and she could see the cords in his neck straining, but that was quickly forgotten when he raised his leg and planted one foot on the couch, his thigh taut and strained as he changed his angle, his cock filling her with pulsing bursts of pleasure.

I can say whatever I want to him, can't I?

That was a delirious thing—something she'd always wondered about. Dirty talk with her husband was a restricted, limited experience that made both of them feel awkward. She'd been subjected to the occasional disgusting message on social media; a guy deciding to say something shocking just to get a response. But she'd never done it. She'd never had the chance.

Or the confidence.

She looped her arms around Levi's neck and pulled him closer. "Come on," she said to him. "Make me cum harder than Woods did. Show me how much you love this pussy."

"Don't—" Levi panted. "Don't talk."

"What's the matter? I thought you weren't going to take it easy on me?"

"I said, *don't talk.*" He repeated the words flatly, leaning his hips forward so that his cock shoved into her so far it hurt, making her wince, and she could feel it flexing inside of her as he came, the warm liquid coating her walls.

"Big Levi. Couldn't handle me. You poor baby," she teased. He withdrew from her, shaking his head.

"Just you wait, Essie. Just you wait."

She rolled onto her side, relishing the pleasant, warm glow of endorphins as she caught her breath. She locked eyes with Woods, who hadn't moved.

"Jealous yet?" she asked.

He sounded amused. "I'm enjoying this new side of you."

She positioned herself so that her legs were sticking in the air, her head hanging upside down, hair stretching to the floor as she taunted him. "Please, Woods. I need it again. Come over here and fuck this pussy again. Spit in it, fuck it until it hurts. It's yours, daddy. You can have whatever you want."

Woods was unperturbed. "Is that all you got?"

She felt Owen's eyes on her. He was still in the corner. Of all the men, he seemed most attached to the costumes. He wore the mask, obviously, but the gloves had stayed firmly on his hands. He was enjoying the show she'd been putting on. Essie sauntered over to him, looking back at Woods and grinning broadly.

She wanted Woods feral. Frothing at the mouth with inflamed jealousy, desperate to prove that he was better than the others.

We all want to be picked, right Woods? We all want that

person to stop and grab us out of a crowd and declare that you—only you—are the one for them.

Her hands sliding down Owen's chest. His posture stiffening, enjoying her touch, her attention. She loved how each of these men came alive whenever she focused on them, their demeanors changing so drastically, each of them ecstatic to have her eyes on them.

She stepped into him, placing her knee between his legs, her hips firm against his waist. He was a bit taller than her; she had to stand slightly on her tiptoes to reach his face with her mouth. She kissed the mask, leaving a messy red lipstick mark. "It's not fair, making you go last," she said to him, letting her voice drip with mock-sadness. "You've been so good, waiting your turn. You deserve a reward, don't you?"

"I do," he replied. His arms gathered around her, rubbing her back until one hand squeezed her ass, drawing a smile from her.

Of all the men, Owen was still the most reserved.

Woods was liable to steal her away for the rest of her life.

Levi clearly wanted her in a hungry, primal way...

But Owen?

He still hadn't moved. Levi would be inside of her by now, and Woods would be saying something filthy in her ear. Owen had a reluctance, a hesitancy. Normally, that would have sparked an insecurity in Essie. Didn't he want her?

But now, in the middle of the hotel suite, with morning sunlight bursting through the half-closed curtains, it made her ravenous for him.

She wanted to see him break.

Essie ran her palm smoothly down his flat stomach, diving under the waistband of his boxers until she felt the beginnings of his trimmed pubic hair. He tensed, the back of his head hitting the wall with a dull thud, his thighs pitching forward as if he were unconsciously drawn to her touch.

"Oh, Owen honey, you are so hard for me." Her fingers wrapped tightly over the base of his cock. She stroked it in short, firm bursts. One-two, one-two—his skin warm, the friction building as he grew harder and harder. "I was going to ask you to turn me around and fuck me against this wall but... I think I can make you cum with just my hand." She squeezed him, drawing a gasp. "Oh, I can *definitely* make you cum." She increased her tempo, twisting her wrist as she stroked him, her hand punching against the inside of his boxers. One-two, one-two. "You've all been toying with me this whole time." She stopped, spit into her hand, and resumed torturing him, hooking her fingers around the waistband and pulling them down, exposing his cock. Her grip slid to the tip of his cock as she placed her thumb against the smooth skin of the head, rubbing it back and forth, all while giving him an innocent, placating smile. "Spanking me, slapping me around, choking me... that's fine. You all *love* that. But I make a little eye contact and tell you to cum for me, and you get shy?" She glanced back at Woods. His expression was blank.

Call me on the bluff, Woods. You know this is all an act. I have no idea what I'm doing. How does someone "be sexy?" I feel like I'm putting on a stage play, like I'm dragging out lines a pornstar would half-mumble before her scene. Get over here and get me out of it, please, before I make a fool of myself. You've talked to me enough, you know I'm not this person.

I just really, really need you to like me.

They each watched her intently, driving the performance anxiety into a sense of power, fueling her desire to do well, to perform for them.

She shoved herself against Owen's chest, coiling her legs around him, stroking his cock faster than ever. Her voice lowered into a sarcastic, bemused tone as she hurled a torrent of words at him, anything and everything to get him to cum. Both of his hands reached around her and her ass and squeezed, lifting her onto her toes again, pulling her tighter to him. "Why aren't you cumming for me?" she said. "I've been such a good girl for you. Come on. Do you want me to beg? I'll beg you. Please give me that cum. I'll let you do anything you want to me. *Please.* You can fuck my throat until I pass out—"

The line occurred to her spur of the moment. Just one of those things she'd picked up from a stray social media post when her algorithm started to get a bit risqué, but it must have caught Owen off guard because he moaned so loudly that Levi heard it and sniggered.

He erupted in her hands, his cum thick and hot.

Essie giggled. "Maybe I should give you guys some safe words. Ya know, since you can't handle me."

She expected Woods to charge across the room. Throw her onto the carpet and fuck her into the floor. She wanted rug burn. She wanted her nails to be raw from gripping the ground.

Woods did the first part. He lunged across the room,

even as Owen was still spurting in her hand. He snatched the chain around her neck and dragged her into the bathroom. "What? Did I do something wrong?"

"Shut up," he ordered. "Take a shower. You have five minutes."

"What? I don't—black card. I'm confused."

He blinked. Then he smiled reassuringly. "Sorry! I was in the moment. You take a break, we will clean up, and we'll have some more fun." He held his mask in his hands, twirling it. "Sorry about the confusion. I was being dominant or whatever. I thought that's what you wanted."

She was burning with embarrassment. For him, for her. Essie had managed to kill the mood in one moment of doubt. "No, you were great. I'm sorry, I misread things—" Now *she* was apologizing, the electricity rapidly draining out of the air, the entire situation feeling more like a fender bender and less like an erotic escape.

"Stop! I swear to God, one more 'sorry' and I'm never getting an erection again." He opened the door and leaned out. "Five minutes! Don't make us come and get you." He said the last part with an edge in his voice that made her bite her lip.

Then he was gone, the door snapping closed behind him, leaving her alone to shower.

There was still soap on her skin when they took her.

The hot water lulled her into a stupor as it pounded on her back—letting her thoughts drift to Woods, to this weekend, to this entire whirlwind of an experience. It was as though her personality was slipping, new pathways opening before her and all she needed was the push to take a new way. There was guilt, too, because she'd never said anything like that in bed with Ryan. She had never taken control. If she had, would they still be okay? Would he have stayed interested in her?

Doesn't matter now.

It didn't, but there was still this lingering attachment to her old life. Kara had returned home a changed, decisive woman. So firm. Her entire life, altered. She had severed the old and drove off into the new. Why didn't Essie feel the same way? The pinballing emotions had to stop. She kept trying to embrace this new, sexual person that Woods wanted to pull out of her, but the tethers were not severing easily.

The door opened. She froze, then called out, "I'll be done in a second!"

The shower curtain shrieked as it was torn aside. Woods, Levi, and Owen were all in the room. The masks were on. So were their gloves. Woods had her phone.

"Your husband has been calling," he said.

Levi and Owen closed in on her, grabbing her and dragging her out of the shower. Owen held her by the hips, lifting her off the floor as Levi held her in a headlock. They carried her out into the living room.

The boys had been busy.

All of the furniture had been shoved against the wall. In the center of the room stood a lone black office chair. The kind that spun. Next to it, maybe four feet away, was a small coffee table. A variety of sex toys were on it.

117

Some of them, like the dildos, she knew what they were. Others, she was less sure about. A roll of tape sat next to the toys, like an ominous threat.

"You," Woods said, "are going to pay for your little stunt earlier."

She squirmed in their grasp, but they ignored her. Woods held the back of the chair still as Owen and Levi made her kneel on it, spreading her knees and sticking her ass out. Levi shoved her forward, her chin resting on the part where your head would normally rest. It reminded her of a stockade; the old wooden things where you stuck your arms and head through so your friends could take pictures.

Her phone rang again.

"This fucking guy," Woods muttered. To the men, he said, "Tape her to the chair."

Levi held her in place, backwards on the chair, as Owen stretched the tape around her. It stuck to her back and shoulders as he looped it around her in one solid band. When he was done, he tore off the end. Her arms could still move—enough to reach behind her a little— and she could move her head to look around, but she was very, very helpless.

So far, the men hadn't done anything too extreme to her. They were rough in the best ways and Woods was keen to make sure she was okay.

But that didn't stop her heart from racing. Or a low moan from escaping her lips when one of them slid a gloved finger into her from behind.

It was Woods. "Already fucking wet? Jesus Christ." He walked in front of her, so she could see the mask as he crouched next to her.

"Just wet from the shower. Nothing to do with you," she shot back.

He seemed like he was about to say something, the mask making him somehow more innocent, when the phone rang for a third time. He showed it to her. "Him again. You're going to answer. All you're going to say is 'let me call you back in a minute.' Understand?"

"I—"

The whip, making another surprise appearance, hissed through the air and cracked against her ass.

"It moves a lot when she's bent over like that," Levi remarked. She felt his hands on her, spreading her ass cheeks apart, working then back and forth and laughing.

The humiliation and social anxiety, the feeling of all of their eyes on her, sent her heart into overdrive, pumping adrenaline and endorphins throughout her body. She was exhilarated, thrilled, terrified... and so, so fucking wet.

"Essie, I need you to say, 'yes sir,' or you'll get it again."

"Yes, sir."

"Good." He paused, running his fingers along the tape. "If this gets uncomfortable, let me know."

Levi approached and handed something to Woods. It was a white device, with a rubber head and a sort of remote attached. Woods turned it over in his hands. "Have you ever used a wand, Essie?"

She had. Carly had talked her into one, describing in great, lurid detail how insane it felt. Essie had spent too much money on one—just to activate it, press it against herself. and immediately turn it off. Some things were too much. "I have, but I'm sensitive so I don't really like them..."

"We'll make you like it," Woods replied. He activated it, the steady *brrrr* noise filling the room like a curious bumblebee. He handed it back to Levi, who went behind her and stuck it underneath her, making her sit on it.

The rubber head fluttered against her pussy—a dull, pulsating pressure that made her whimper and raise her thighs to keep from putting her full weight down on it.

"Turn it down lower," Woods said.

Levi squeezed her ass, but a moment later, the *brrrr* quieted to a dull hum. She was able to rest on the wand, letting it vibrate against her, but only for a few seconds before she had to raise herself again. The result was a maddening, pleasure-agony game of stamina. She kept dipping back down, kissing it briefly with her pussy, then raising up to get a break.

All while the masked men watched, and her husband called her cellphone.

On the third ring, Woods tapped it and held it to her ear. Levi was talking to Owen in the background, the wand was humming cheerfully against her clit, and Woods was staring into her soul.

She hated her husband so much.

"Let me call you back," she rasped, even as he started to ask questions.

"Hey Essie, wha—"

Woods hung up the phone. "You'll call back in a second."

She squirmed. The wand was warm now, and getting comfortable against her. Too comfortable. It was starting to feel incredible. "I will?"

"Yes. With all three of us inside of you."

They backed away, assembling in a loose triangle around her. Woods was to her left, Owen to her right. Out of her periphery, she could see Levi, tilting his head and staring intently at her ass.

"Who wants to spin her?" Woods asked.

Spin?

No one answered, but two black gloved hands appeared at her sides, gripping the arm rests of the chair. With a grunt, one of the men sent her spinning in the chair, rotating once, twice, three times until she was facing Owen. He began unbuckling his belt.

The wand kept vibrating. Her thighs ached; she wouldn't be able to keep off of it much longer. If she rested on it, it would make her cum immediately.

"Guess you get her mouth," Woods said casually. "Levi? Rock, paper, scissors for her ass?"

I hate him. I'm sure of it. I hate him so much.

"You can have it," Levi replied. "I want to feel that pussy again."

They converged on her. One of them reached down to the lever on the base of the chair and lowered it, sinking her in front of Owen, who lazily pulled out his cock and slapped it against her face. The wand rolled with the movement of the chair, slipping higher, now thrumming directly against her clit, working back and forth like an aggressive tongue.

"*Fffffuck*" Essie groaned.

"We haven't even fucked you yet," Woods teased.

Their hands were firm and hungry as they each felt up her body. She lost track of who was where, as all six seemed intent on touching her simultaneously. One pinched her nipples. Another pulled her hair. Her ass was smacked over and over. A finger slipped inside of her, increasing the pressure from the wand. Someone's thumb rubbed her asshole. Owen leaned down, lifted the mask, and spit on her face. Large hands ran down her back and squeezed her hips appreciatively. She was choked and told to pucker her lips for Levi's cock. Or maybe it was Owen's? She lost track, caught between the lust of the three men, each of them wanting her to look at them while they fucked her, each of them wanting her *so* badly.

One of their voices told her she was worthless, that this is where she belonged, servicing them. Another voice told her how goddamned good she looked, that they couldn't believe they got to do this to her.

She was their angel and their whore.

Someone clicked the wand and it vibrated furiously, making her squeal, but Owen told her to shut the fuck up as he stuffed his cock down her throat.

Behind her, the sound of a plastic container being uncapped, then a long trail of a warm liquid dripped into her ass, followed by a finger—teasing her, before slowly sliding in, drawing a feral, animalistic noise from her.

Woods appeared next to her again, even as Owen's cock pumped against her cheek. She could only move her eyes; Owen held her head firmly in place. Levi shoved himself into her from behind, saying, "This is the wettest pussy I've ever felt." He sounded impressed.

Woods, calmly, raised the phone to her ear. It rang once.

"You have Owen's cock in your mouth," Woods said.

It rang again.

"You have Levi's in your pussy," he added.

It rang once more.

"And you have my finger in your ass." He said the last one with a smile, and slid it in deeper, making her gasp, drawing Owen's cock down her throat, making her gag violently. Owen pulled it out, saliva spilling out, coating her mouth and chin.

The phone rang again.

"Is this what you wanted, Essie?" Woods asked. He was almost whispering, his eyes very bright. "When you called us, is this what you wanted?"

"Yes. God, yes," she gasped.

The phone clicked. Ryan answered. "Hey honey, I'm glad you called back!"

Levi slammed his cock into her, burying it to the hilt before withdrawing and jackhammering it back into her, putting his entire weight behind it—she could even feel the front of his thighs flexing.

Woods slid the entire length of his finger into her ass, the shock of pleasure and discomfort fusing with that sense of being *filled*, of being *f-u-c-k-e-d* making her collapse onto the angry head of the wand, which assaulted her clit and sent a torrent of sensation through her, all while Owen traced the outline of her mouth with his cock.

Essie no longer cared if her ex-husband—*yes, yes he's my ex there's no going back now*—heard what was happening. The phone was firm against her ear, but she spoke to Woods instead.

"Please don't stop."

Ryan's baffled voice, full of questions, faded from her as Woods took the phone away. He stood back up and held it to his ear. Essie, bouncing back and forth from the force of Levi, looked up at him.

"She's busy right now," he said pleasantly. He hung up the phone and tossed it away. He looked down at her, smiling.

Then he put the white mask back on.

CHAPTER 10

They kept her a bit longer than they planned, Woods told her. This was after she'd been laid flat on the floor, wearing Wood's mask as the wand continued to torture her, letting the men cum all over the mask.

The ride home, which she'd been dreading, was just as eventful as the ride to the hotel. Woods made the others sit in the front, and he and Essie laid in the back like teenagers hiding from their parents. They laid on their backs while the road bumped and jostled beneath them.

Woods took a deep breath, as if preparing for a

speech. He handed her a card, a white one. It was for the hotel, but on the back, he'd scribbled a phone number. "You're annoying," he said, "and I don't really know how a relationship between us would work, or if you'd even want one, but I like you. If things don't work out between you and your husband and... You know, you take your time to heal and all that—"

She laughed. "Is that your move? Tell girls they're annoying then ask them out?"

"No, I just throw them in my van."

"Do they like that?"

"The slutty ones do," he said.

"So I'm annoying *and* slutty."

He covered her mouth with his hand and she licked it, causing a mild wrestling match that ended in wild, sleep-deprived laughter.

A silence fell as she turned the card over in her hands. It had his name, and with a jolt she realized it was the first time learning his first name.

Leslie Woods.

Essie held the card up as if it were a fake one-hundred dollar bill, examining it in the dim light of the van. "Your name is Leslie?" she asked, repressing a giggle.

"Family name," he muttered. "Shut up."

"It's cute. So, is all of this—" she gestured at the van "—a way of overcompensating for your girly name?"

"You know what? Give me that back. I'm not taking you out on a date—"

She curled her fingers around it as he pulled her closer to him. "Nope," she said. "It's mine."

"Your name is stupid, too. What the fuck is Essie—"

"It's short for Esmerelda."

"That's not fair. That's really hot." He kissed her firmly—one of those long, searching kisses that felt dangerously like something real.

It was late; easily after midnight. Ryan would be asleep. He'd called a few times, but she'd been very, very busy. Her entire body was sore and aching and she wanted to sleep for a week.

But there was one, final thing she wanted. She turned on her side and curled up next to Woods. She whispered in his ear what she wanted, her final black card request. His eyes widened, but he said he would do it.

Essie let herself back into her own house, creeping through the darkness like a burglar. She closed the door as quietly as possible, set down her bag, kicked off her shoes, and tiptoed through the living room, down the hallway to the bedroom.

The light was on.

Ryan was lying in bed, reading a book. He glanced up at her, his face set in pre-prepared anger. "Do you want to explain what the fuck happened this weekend?"

"No." She climbed on to the bed and on top of him, giving him a sloppy, eager kiss. He grunted, his hands automatically moving down her body.

"What is going on with you—" he muttered, but she ignored him as she seized him by the hair and gripped the headboard with her free hand. He got the message and pulled off her shorts; the very shorts she'd been kidnapped in.

Essie sat on her husband's face and felt his mouth embrace her pussy. For once, he was using a lot of tongue.

Woods' cum began to leak out of her. She could feel it; it was still warm.

He'd been fucking her until about a block from her house.

Ryan tasted it. She felt him pause. "Essie, there's something, uh, coming out of you—"

She grinded down on his mouth as hard as she could.

"I want a divorce," she said.

ACKNOWLEDGEMENTS

Big thanks to Molly, The Havoc Archives, cover artist Charlyy, all the beta readers and ARC readers, my dearest Magneto for their unwavering support, Julie for all her help in the drafting phase, and Megan for her help with graphics and promo.

Big NO thank you to my day job. I hate you and you suck.

ABOUT THE AUTHOR

JD Midnight is from Michigan and lives near a cemetery.

He thinks about the cemetery a lot.

ALSO BY
JD MIDNIGHT

Caution Tape w/Molly Doyle
Body Count w/Molly Doyle
Reverie, Reverie, Reverie.
September Bleeds October (releasing 2024)

Made in United States
Troutdale, OR
05/05/2025

31096837R00080